Our Perfect Murder

Camille Cabrera

Our Perfect Murder. Copyright © 2023 Camille Cabrera.

All rights reserved.

No part of this book can be reproduced in any form without the written permission of the author.

This is a work of fiction. The characters and events in this book are fiction and from the author's imagination. Any resemblance to actual persons, living or dead, locales or events is completely coincidental.

Dedication:

To all the little girls that were told that they were too outspoken for the world. Take up space.

Cultivate your power.

More Books By Camille Cabrera:

Catalina's Tide

The Rule of Three

Chronometer

Below The Water

Live so passionately that you scare your demons.

Chapter 1

"I didn't kill her."

Detective Godford arched a dark eyebrow in obvious skepticism as he hunkered deeper into the metal chair. Pictures of the crime scene littered the table like a macabre jigsaw puzzle. His arctic gray eyes gave little away, but Ember already knew that she was in mierda.

Deep mierda.

If her grandmother was seated in the interrogation room, she'd make the sign of the cross and tell her only granddaughter that her best chance at redemption would be to kneel on the concrete ground and pray away all of her sins. It was a task that would likely take a minimum of four to six business days. Not that Ember had that kind of time.

"You've said that, Ms. Lopez. Would you like to shed some light on why you're so sure of that statement?"

Sweat made Ember's palms sticky as she absently rubbed them on her faded blue jeans. Her gaze traveled to the large one-way window. The fact that the small town of Ashburn had an interrogation room equally impressed and terrified her. Of course, having spoken with the sheriff several times at the local diner, the traces of his poorly hidden paranoia were as obvious as his addiction to his morning cup of burning black coffee. The townspeople knew that the sheriff was famous for giving folks unnecessary trouble on days when he had skipped his morning cup of Joe. It put him in a bad mood and often made him more unfriendly than usual. If that was even possible.

"Anytime, Ms. Lopez."

The detective's clipped words quickly brought Ember back to the present moment. Her palms were drenched with sweat.

"Right. It all started about two years ago when I listened to my first true-crime podcast and thought that they had done a horrible job. Don't get me wrong, the case was intriguing, but their assumptions were sloppy and it was obvious that they had rushed their research. It was too commercial. Too impersonal. There was no passion or genuine curiosity."

"Not how you started your podcast. A podcast which now has over 20,000 listeners since the murder of Mrs. Westin."

Ember visibly bristled at the detective's surliness. His clipped tone held an edge of smugness and it made her want to hit him.

Hard.

She daydreamed about giving him a firm slap to the face. Still, that was not the same as committing or even daydreaming about murder.

Ember straightened her posture and spoke in a clipped manner, "I didn't kill someone for 19,975 podcast followers if that's the motive you've decided to pin on me."

"I never mentioned a motive. I also never said that you were a suspect in an ongoing investigation, but if you feel like you need legal representation then a lawyer can be provided to you."

He slowly leaned back in the metallic chair. Detective Godford arched a superior thick eyebrow, intended to indicate a challenge.

Ember watched the intentionally inciting movement and wished that there was the slightest puddle of water directly under one of those budget-friendly metal chair legs. Obviously not hoping that he'd die, but hoping that the impact would humble him just enough to bring down his ego. Ember was already in enough trouble for murder.

No such luck. The detective's chair remained steadily in place.

Usually, Ember didn't consider herself a violent person, but the entire situation had put her on the defensive. She felt like a caged animal as the man across from her tried to connect her to a murder that she definitely didn't commit.

She was nervous, but in a much deeper sense she was also furious. Ember was willing to empty the sparse amount of money left in her checking account just to watch Detective Godford's ego get pummeled down a peg or two. He was too smug and his face was just too perfect. White-hot frustration coursed through Ember's veins. This unreasonably handsome man was toying with her. Raking her belly through the coals just to see if she had any secrets left to share.

The jerk had another thing coming if he thought that a few harsh sentences could bully her into admitting to committing murder. Ember had attended a public school in Los Angeles, in one of the rougher districts. Now that was hard.

At the end of the day, verbal threats weren't exactly the ones that ruffled Ember's feathers. She could deal with words. Unlike the common saying, sticks and stones really hurt when kids in the schoolyard were hurling them at your head.

Ember tossed her hands up into the air in mounting frustration. Her lower lip curled back in revulsion. Ember appeared as if she had just tasted something particularly bitter, "We both know what it looks like. It's a shaky motive to pin on me and you know it! We both know that if you really had anything on me, then I'd already be under arrest. I've researched enough actual crimes for my podcast to know that much."

Ember paused. She allowed just enough time to catch her breath, but no more. She then continued, "Look, we both know that this makes me look very bad, but I promise you last night I watched reality television and ate an entire can of whipped cream by myself. That's it."

Suddenly, a hard fist slammed against the thick metal door. Three loud pounds in quick succession. Before Detective Godford could call out a response, a member of the police station bustled into the room. The newcomer held out a folded sheet of paper. The paper had clearly been hastily ripped away from the spine of a notebook.

Detective Godford gave the note an inquisitive cursory glance and thanked the lumbering man that hovered a few inches away from the table. The balding man gave Ember a generous amount of side-eye.

Detective Godford's gaze scanned the note several times. A deep frown caused the top of his tanned forehead to crumple.

"Let me guess, you found out that I ditched class in 2011 to go see a Joana Sister's Concert? Is that an arrestable offense?"

Ember's statement dripped with sarcasm. She had decided from the start that her best defense was a witty combination of sarcasm and sass.

The room was cloaked in a heavy, nearly unbearable silence. The weight pressed down against Ember's chest and made it difficult for her to breathe. The anxiety in her body continued to grow. It felt like a ginormous rat was skulking around the dark corners of her mind. Gnawing at the last vestiges of her mental comfort.

Detective Godford kept his eyes trained on the page as if the secret to eternal life was scrawled across the crooked piece of unimpressive scratch paper. Eventually, he refolded the note along the same crooked crease.

His throat bobbed as he thickly swallowed down what appeared to be his pride. He mumbled, "You're free to go, Ms. Lopez."

Ember blinked, "What? Just like that? Didn't you just say that I should get a lawyer? What changed?"

The questions shot from Ember's mouth in quick succession. She folded her arms over her chest and narrowed her eyes in disbelief. This had to be a trick. A way to pry a false confession from her lips.

Detective Godford pinched the bridge of his nose and inhaled deeply. Once he appeared slightly more composed he said, "There's been another murder. You better leave this room, Ms. Lopez, before I decide to take you into custody for unruly behavior."

It seemed like an empty threat, but Ember wasn't in the mood to take any chances. She silently stood from the metal seat and waited in vain for answers that wouldn't come.

How annoying.

Chapter 2

Ember often found herself curious to the point of painful stupidity. As a school child, she had frequently gotten in trouble because she always stuck her nose in places where it didn't belong. The idea that a teacher would ever grow exasperated with questions had never occurred to Ember. Not until her first grade teacher Mrs. Shambles had publicly embarrassed her for being a precocious, Nosy Nelly.

Unfortunately, the childish nickname had stuck. Ember had missed out on countless birthday parties and sleepovers. The entrance of a new kid had finally elevated her social standing by one person. She had had to climb out of the social pariah ditch on the back of an extremely introverted foreign-exchange student. Ember had learned that people frequently bullied or harassed others for their differences. Unfortunately, Ember had never figured out how to hide her quirks.

Eventually, the class had reluctantly invited her into their fold. The threat of a newcomer had motivated them to close rank. The realization did little to quell Ember's fury at the injustice and after three months of enjoying multiple friendships and sleepovers, she had eventually caved and invited the new girl over to her grandmother's house for a play date. Ember had remembered what it felt like to be all alone. She decided to gamble her own tiny social standing on the playground in the hopes of helping the miserable French girl. Unsurprisingly, it had cost Ember a seat at every single lunch table for an entire year. The isolation didn't really bother Ember since the stairs to the classroom were the perfect makeshift table for her and Eloise to enjoy recess. Ember had lost the temporary favor of her classmates in exchange for a permanent friendship. It was a good trade in her book.

    As she got older, Ember had struggled to refrain from constantly asking a mountain of questions in class. She had often contented herself with the small tidbits of information provided by the teachers. After class, Ember had often studiously searched for answers to the list of questions that she had written down during the school day. Although her teachers had made her afraid of asking questions, they hadn't squelched her curiosity. Her constant curiosity had simply been subverted to the underground. Maybe that deep yearning to understand the world never disappeared with age. Maybe that's why Ember had decided to start that stupid podcast in the first place.

    Idiot.

    Ember returned back to the moment and glanced around the interrogation room with a blank stare. It was so intentionally ugly and devoid of life that Ember had thought that she was likely facing a minimum of 20 years in the slammer. Without another word, Ember stood from her seat and headed for the door. She told herself to keep her mouth shut. The morning replayed on a constant loop in the back of her mind as she placed one foot in front of the other. Before she reached the door, Detective Godford prodded, "You're not even a little curious as to what happened?"

For once, an easy truth slid past her previously pursed lips, "I learned that the people that ask too many questions end up getting questioned by townie cops. I don't want to know anymore than what you have offered the public."

"Liar."

"It takes one to know one, Detective Godford." Ember sneered out his title with a generous helping of disdain.

Detective Godford clutched the note within his left palm as the sound of crumpling paper filled the cramped space. He took great effort to unwrinkle the precious sliver of notebook paper. Obviously, he was easier to upset than Ember had originally thought. Good.

His gaze held none of the ferocity that Ember had previously predicted. Instead, Detective Godford's face remained passive. Only a single furiously pulsing vein near the bottom of his neck gave away his rising anger. Molten quicksilver never glanced away from verdant green.

"All you need to know is that you have been released from police custody for the time being. That is, unless you would prefer to stay."

He was teasing her. The implications from the persistent questions were clear. Ember was still a top suspect.

"I'll be going." Ember placed her hand on the door handle, but paused as a deep voice laced with warning called, "Oh, Ember?"

"What?"

"Don't talk about this on your podcast."

A bitter scoff escaped the back of Ember's throat as she mumbled under her breath, "That's what got me into this mess in the first place."

Chapter 3

"Clean up on Aisle Three."

The voice of Ember's nearly pubescent coworker rang across the store. Not that the store was large enough to require a microphone system. A gutsy yell was more than enough to travel the length of the establishment.

William continued his monologue about the dozen or so daily deals that more realistically changed weekly. The store only claimed to have daily deals in an effort to motivate people to buy more. However, that tactic didn't seem to work. The entire town realistically only shopped in one place. People loved to go to the shop and talk. The entire town knew the items were weekly deals, but that didn't stop the store owner from trying to pass them off as daily specials.

Al, the owner of the shop received the best bargain values on an assortment of items because of sly resourcing and an unusual lack of competition. Realistically, he had some bargain busters that were too good to be true. Ember always had a sneaking suspicion that Al had a source that worked in one of the various food packaging centers. What the area lacked in might, it definitely made up for in factories and processing plants. There were at least six factories within a ten-mile radius of the sleepy little town. The area had major factories that produced products like canned corn. Somehow Al's store always managed to have a cutthroat competitive price on the product. Ember had a hunch that the price had very little to do with the store's close location to the factory.

The nuances of the town didn't bother Ember. Overall, she was just grateful to be away from the big city. Years ago, Ember had told herself that the pace was much too fast and chaotic to properly relax. She swore that cities were designed for people that were dependent on finding the next big thing for amusement. Usually, people in the City of Angels dreamt a common dream that centered around international stardom. Of course, the number of people that were actually plucked from anonymity and thrust into the spotlight was slim, but that didn't stop every waiter and nanny from trying.

The collective wishful thinking was just another reason on Ember's long list of reasons to leave Los Angeles.

"It's good to see you, Ember!"

A woman in her mid-60s waddled near. She smiled but the awkward action managed to scrunch her facial features in the wrong order. It was as if she was having a difficult time remembering the steps to forming a genuine grin.

Mrs. Bloomsworth held a small shopping basket full of microwavable toaster strudels and continued, "I am so happy to have run into you, Dear. We simply must do something about your lawn. I noticed that the blades of grass at your rental are getting a little long and they're nearing the maximum limit of three inches. I'm only reminding you so that you don't need to pay the fee that will likely be extremely burdensome for you."

Normally, Mrs. Bloomsworth's behavior angered Ember on a similar level to how a buzzing fly annoyed a horse. Constant, but typically easy to ignore. Unfortunately, Ember had just spent four hours at the police station getting all manner of invasive questions thrown in her direction.

"Thank you so much, Mrs. Bloomsworth. It's inexplicable to have a neighbor like you."

Ember leveled the older woman with a hard stare as her words failed to hit the intended target. The thinly veiled insult managed to roll off Mrs. Bloomsworth's back like water off a duck.

"Absolutely, Doll. Don't forget to start planning for the Valentine's Day Parade."

Mercifully, Mrs. Bloomsworth's microscopic attention span jumped to a different train of thought. Her aged gaze shifted from Ember's face and tracked Al down as he entered the store. Just like that, the conversation ended as Mrs. Bloomsworth left Ember standing in the middle of the aisle.

"Valentine's Day is a week away and I already hate it. What a stupid holiday," Ember muttered. She returned her attention back to the restocking and redesigning of a pyramid made out of bargain-brand cans of soup. The bright red cans worked perfectly with the upcoming holiday theme.

    Subtle whispers caught Ember's attention as she strained her ears to hear bits and pieces of the conversation. Usually, Ember tried to let other people have their privacy, but in all fairness, she had already heard her name mentioned three times. The odds of another person being called Ember that she didn't already know about in a town of 3,000 people were basically negative.

    Ember held the price gun up a few inches away from the cans as she listened. The women sounded older. One of the voices already held that deeper rasp that so often emerged in the back of an individual's throat over time. Of course, Ember loathed the idea that a person that had truly lived a meaningful life would so excitedly gossip about a woman several decades her minor.

    "Do you think that they'll put her away or have her committed?"

    "Goodness, I am sure that they will have no choice. She is clearly a danger to the community. It's just a matter of time before she grows brave and does it again. Next time, she might select someone more irreplaceable from our town and then the community will never recover."

    Mrs. Van Scorn tended to have an extremely distinct nasally voice that effortlessly carried within any tightly confined space. Ember closed her eyes and imagined how the gray-haired town crier would have clutched her pearls in fake distress at the idea of someone meaningful being killed. As if every life wasn't in itself precious. The women all gasped with poorly executed fake shows of concern. The people Mrs. Van Scorn considered important, tended to vary depending on her needs. It often depended on who could best keep up with her theatrical meltdowns.

Ember's mind unwillingly pulled her back to a memory dredged from the depths of her subconscious. When Ember had first arrived in town, Mrs. Van Scorn had swiftly assumed the role of a matriarchal figure for Ember.

Ember had unwittingly been taken under the wing of the town's most vicious gossip. As a young and impressionable individual, Ember had blindly accepted the misleading gesture of kindness. At first, Mrs. Van Scorn had asked Ember to fetch a small carton of milk for the block party. The older woman had been too busy with other activities to get it herself. Slowly, the favors and random expenses had grown too burdensome and unreasonable.

Unfortunately, Ember had been like a frog in a boiling pot of hot water. She hadn't noticed how manipulative Mrs. Van Scorn was until it was too late. Of course, once she had finally put her foot down Mrs. Van Scorn had promptly buried Ember's reputation with lies.

Overnight, the entire town had effectively turned its back on Ember by Mrs. Van Scorn's high-pitched decree. To hear the woman that she had once viewed as a mother-like figure gossiping about her just one aisle down hurt like a reopened wound. Of course, she wasn't exactly surprised.

Ember had been cast out of town society from the moment that she had told Mrs. Van Scorn no. Five years later, the bad blood was still there and appeared thicker than ever. The town members now rarely spoke to Ember unless they needed help finding the right product. It came as no surprise that the town had easily believed that she was trouble. Ember hadn't been given a trial, but the people that she lived with had already declared her guilty beyond a reasonable doubt. Damn, Ember hoped that they would never actually be on a jury panel.

The final part of her chest that was still untarnished by the heartache seemed to wither away at the last betrayal. Ember had foolishly hoped that people would at least have the decency to ask her for more details about the ongoing case.

The price sticker gun buzzed into overdrive as yellow flecks of paper whirled from the machine and flew into the air. The colored stickers spewed out like confetti and covered the items on the shelves in a particularly haphazard manner. A loud whine wound into the air as the machine kicked up another notch.

Immediately, the squabbling coming from the other women stopped. A forced hush blanketed the previously noisy aisle just inches away. Mortified wasn't the right word to describe Ember's frazzled emotions as she grappled for purchase along the extremely rocky shores of her own dignity. From the officers down at the station to the rubbernecking ladies at the mart, it was abundantly clear that she was the oddball in town. It only made sense that she'd be the first one that they would try to convict of murder. Tears welled in the back of Ember's eyes. She didn't have any friends and she was a loner. Ember refused to cry. Instead, she turned her gaze to the left and met three painted gaping mouths.

    Awesome.

    Ember walked in the group's direction. Unsurprisingly, the trio of gossiping faces scurried out of her way like frightened mice running away from a starved barn cat. A ghost of a smile played at the edges of Ember's chapped lips as she kept her back to the women. She used her back like a makeshift shield. She couldn't handle any more questioning glances. Not today.

    A lone tear trickled down the side of Ember's face, but she quickly wiped away the traitorous reaction with the back of her hand. The movement caused her to press more deeply into the trigger of the price gun. Another explosion of colorful paper escaped the confines of the plastic gun and elicited a string of panicked shrieks from surrounding customers.

Automated front doors swung open and a blast of crisp February air wrapped around the dark exposed hairs along Ember's arms. Sure, she needed a job, but she wasn't about to ignore the fury and mounting horror bubbling within her gut.

For today, she still had enough pride to walk away. It was a desperate and likely futile effort to save the little remaining bits of her quickly crumbing decorum.

"Don't cry, Mamacita. Estoy fuerte," The words and positive self-talk did little to bolster Ember's nerves, but at least she had tried her best. Perhaps some situations were a little too complex for simple platitudes.

"Ember! You just started your shift! You need to come back right now!"

Mr. Bleeker waddled out of the store with flushed cheeks and an obvious sheen of sweat reflected along his receding hairline. For a moment, Ember looked back and felt absolutely horrible for her boss. That was until she remembered that he had pulled her in last week for double shifts to accommodate his bumbling nephew who decided to have a multi-day movie marathon instead of showing up to work. Usually, a kid taking a few days to blow off some steam didn't bother Ember, but Mr. Bleeker's nephew was 32 and still spent his days hanging out with high schoolers. It felt creepy, to say the least. On Mr. Bleeker's part, he was enabling his kin. Ember was more than ready to tell them both off.

She took in a deep gulp of air and croaked out, "You need more soap on Aisle 2. I quit."

Her slim fingers wrapped around the metal nameplate on her shirt. Ember yanked on it and tossed the simple tag at Mr. Bleeker's feet. The plate had always felt so redundant. It was a place where everyone already knew your name.

Ember sped out of the newly cemented grocery store parking lot and trotted out onto the main road. In the back of her mind, Ember knew that she was definitely too upset to drive. The odds that such a short distance would leave her wrapped around a tree felt closer to a guarantee than a possibility. It wasn't so much of an if as opposed to a when. Ember had sensitive eyes that were easily irritated. Crying made it especially difficult for her to see. The odd problem rarely bothered Ember, but today was not the day for such quirks.

Decided, Ember abandoned her bright red decade-old sedan in the parking lot and vowed to come back for it once the store had officially closed for the night.

A distant voice called from behind, "Ember, you're right! You can have that raise that I promised you last year. How does an extra $0.50 per hour sound?"

It sounded like a fresh load of steaming bullshit. The raise was a slap in the face to all of Ember's time and effort.

An idiotic ploy that Mr. Bleeker enjoyed pulling on a semi-annual basis. The promise of a paltry raise would never actually arrive. The promises often happened around the same time that Ember considered leaving for a different job. Surely even a small town had at least one better gig.

Initially, Ember had desperately needed a source of income to keep her on her feet. She had arrived with only $40 in her pocket and not one townsperson had questioned her decision to set down roots. Retrospectively, the entire situation had been unhinged. Five years later, the idea of finding something else while still living from one paycheck to the next sounded scary, but Ember wasn't exactly known for making the most rational choices.

Her dirtied tennis shoes stomped along the side of the road. A small pebble entered the top of her shoe. It did little to improve Ember's mood as she skulked home, muttering a string of unintelligible curses under her breath.

Ember turned her head to the side and took note of the vast local graveyard. The old graves appeared relatively inviting as bright sunlight beamed against the white and gray-kissed markers. The people in town rarely ventured outside of their daily routines. The graves looked as if they were stacked one on top of the other. It appeared that there were generations of people intertwined in death like vines on a trellis.

The idea of such a deep sense of rooted belonging, stretching back for generations made Ember ache. She could barely remember her mother and she had absolutely no recollection of her father. Ember's mom had always told her that it was a painful subject. As a kid, Ember had begrudgingly accepted the explanation and avoided bringing up her dad. Now, Ember wished that she had pushed a little harder for clues.

Ember grew listless after her mom passed away and eventually floated over to a quaint little town in the middle of nowhere. Ember had randomly received an incorrectly addressed postcard. It displayed a small photo of an idyllic Main Street. The photo had to have been taken during the late spring. The image held bright and vibrant sunflowers that stretched up into the sky from every available flowerbed and street corner. In reality, the postcard had underpromised in terms of flowers. Flowers were common and appeared in every nook and cranny when the weather grew warmer. Any pothole or crack became an opportunity for life to begin as lone sunflowers grew with wild abandon and little regard for city planning. The vibrant colors almost made the hideous potholes bearable.

After the graveyard, Ember walked near the hospital. She had always thought that whoever had designed the hospital rooms to overlook the cemetery deserved to be fired. Either they were thoughtless in their creation or had the sickest sense of humor in the history of city planning. Ember guessed that she would have been excellent friends with such weirdos. Once the hospital was out of sight, the rear section of Main Street came into view. For a relatively early afternoon, the area bustled with more people than usual. Typically, one or two parents sat around drinking coffee or eating outside of the ancient Italian restaurant where grease often dripped down to your elbows after folding a slice of pizza. It was a great place in terms of convenience. Given, the idea of convenience was abstract because the sleepy town often took its time to get anywhere.

    Ember noticed the quaint pharmacy tucked into the corner and glanced at one of the adjacent hair salons. One of the town matriarchs entered the salon for her weekly trim. At first, it had seemed so predictable to have so many women in their late 70s donning the same hairstyle, but Ember had quickly realized that she was being hypocritical. After all, what was the saying? Birds of a feather.

    The entire idyllic scene unsettled Ember's nerves as she watched people go about their daily lives. How were people able to keep living? Didn't they know that someone had just been killed? Ember was in shock as she walked faster down the street. She couldn't believe that she was being questioned for murder. The trap was set and she knew that it was only a matter of time before it fully closed around her.

Chapter 4

The podcast icon flashed to life and Ember quickly lowered the brightness on her old computer screen. A few sections of the screen were permanently cracked into rainbows of various colors. The bright pinks and purples played along the edges of the screen, but Ember couldn't look away from her stupid podcast logo. Her cheerful face peered out from the little logo as she held a cup of coffee in one hand and practically clinked glasses with onlooking viewers. The image of her outstretched mug was the cheery cherry on top. Ember reluctantly noted the skill of the graphic designer that she had hired to achieve such an artistic feat. The podcast logo really did look three-dimensional.

Her entire podcast focused on delving into true crime stories and popular unsolved cases. Why did she ever think that she could have a successful podcast show as an Afro-latina trapped in the middle of a small town in the U.S.A.? Maybe her mom had dropped her one too many times as a baby.

"Stupid. Stupid. You idiota," Ember chastised her poor choices and then decided she had to stop procrastinating. She had no time to lose. Especially now that another person had been murdered. That made dos. Two murders in less than two days. Ember knew that all fingers pointed in her direction. A shiver of unease crept along her spine. Ember had very little to prove her innocence. She just had to run her big mouth. Maybe she'd dig up a few clues down the line. That was a big maybe. Luckily, the sheriff had a loud mouth after a few drinks. A tentative plan formed in the back of Ember's mind as her index finger darted out and slammed the play button on the podcast episode that started it all.

Chapter 5

Good afternoon to anyone and everyone tuning in! A special shout out to listeners close to Sacramento. I'm not exactly located in Sacramento, but that's all I plan to say. After all, a woman can never be too careful about what she puts online. Today, I am going to talk about the string of murders that rocked the small town of Ashburn. The murders surrounding this town always fascinated me because it seemed so obvious to me where the killer messed up. It's not because the cops found the killer. The man that they had held for questioning wasn't egotistical enough for these kills. The townspeople had simply created a feeding frenzy surrounding this one individual because he stuck out like a sore thumb. His differences ultimately put a target on his back. Look, the killer often had a very specific type of victim. His victims were usually women from Ashburn in their late teens to early thirties. These ladies all had futures and were interested in getting ahead in life. Each woman had little in common with the other murdered individuals. Similarities seemed to start and stop with the understanding that the women all came from the same cloistered town. It was a major failure on the part of the investigators to rush arrests. Small towns often have deeply hidden inner workings. The details of how a small community works are not shared with or even clearly understood by outside law enforcement. It's extremely simple to forget that in a town like Ashburn, there is only one hospital and one main grocery store. Small towns let killers hide in blind spots created by familiarity. You're much more likely to feel wary of someone like a stranger heading up your porch when it's close to sundown as opposed to your friendly neighborhood milkman. Such familiarity often encourages people to let their guards down. This killer was in a blindspot and then got too comfortable. He was too confident in his position and eventually messed up. Now, before any listener asks why I said he, the reason is because an overwhelming majority of violent crimes are committed by men. In general, men are responsible for about 98% of all violent crimes worldwide. So the assumption that this killer is a male is more than valid. I'm getting distracted. As I was saying, the killer was too confident. His final known victim, Jessica Spelunky wasn't a local working woman in her 20s. She was a housewife visiting her friend that worked at the local bank. Like I said before, it's a small town so there are only about two financial institutions in town. One is a bank and the other is a credit union. It's very likely that the killer had not intended to murder Jessica Spelunky and instead had intended to kill her friend that she was staying with. It's possible that the killer had gotten confused because the two women had similar features. Jessica Spelunky had been staying at Miranda Melvy's rental. I am willing to bet that the killer took the wrong woman and it drove him crazy. Well, crazier. He's probably still out there right now, simmering and stewing, waiting for his next victim in order to create the perfect murder. From all of the documents that I've read and all of the information that I've collected, this killer was meticulous. He had a strict style that he very clearly preferred. He often first bound his captives and took them to a second location. From the document, it's clear from obvious signs of struggle that the victims were awake. The killer slowly drowned his victims in a way that left them with a minimal amount of water in their lungs. Such a meticulous method leaves an individual relatively preserved. Typically there is a fine window between death and rigor mortis that allows the killer to position his victims. He clearly believed that he'd found the best way to commit murder. With each new victim, the amount of water found within their lungs significantly decreased. In my opinion, he failed to commit the perfect murder. He had left a note at the last scene of the crime claiming it was the perfect murder, but I disagree. A perfect murder would be clean and difficult to catch. I don't know, I suppose that I'm just spitballing now. It's clearly time for me to end this episode, but be sure to listen next week for a deeper dive into this case.

Chapter 6

Ember fervently wished that she had a baseball bat in her home. She fantasized about smashing her second-hand laptop to pieces. Anything to get her own voice to stop ringing inside of her head. How could she have been so stupid?

Suddenly, she bolted from her bargain store folding plastic chair and made a beeline for the bathroom. Bile burned the back of her throat as she released the meager contents of her stomach into the toilet bowl. A sheen of perspiration traced along the edges of her hairline as her skin turned an ashen shade of gray.

She had no idea how long she stayed hugging the toilet. Time no longer mattered. Ember struggled to feel anything outside of an overwhelming sense of self-loathing. A vicious voice in the back of her mind kept screaming at her that both murders were her fault. Ember was too exhausted to argue with the uncaring voice in the back of her mind. She allowed it to condemn her to purgatory. She rubbed a dribble of snot onto the sleeve of her shirt as a second wave of nausea enveloped all of her senses. Ember heaved into the toilet, but very little escaped her lips. She had nothing left to give.

Eventually, Ember shakily sat up as her eyes stared at nothing in particular. She wished that she had never started the damn podcast in the first place. How stupid could she be? Of course, some perverted weirdo would exploit her ideas as well as other innocent women. She did live in the United States, after all.

A soft rapping drew Ember's attention away from the starving black spiral in the back of her mind. The noise was just loud enough to pull her away from the voracious nothingness.

Ember's bleary gaze settled on a persnickety feathered friend that pecked against the small glass window. It had to be around six in the evening. Her pals always came to visit around dinner time.

With the meager strength left in her body, Ember struggled to stand. She shuffled into the kitchen and carried an entire bag of corn outside. Today, it didn't matter if her lovely companions became slightly overfed. It wasn't everyday that a girl accidentally inspired a murder. Possibly two.

Several large crows impatiently hopped around Ember's front yard. Impressively sized black dots crowed in excitement as Ember reached into the corn bag and carelessly tossed out several handfuls of feed. The birds descended on the feast as Ember slumped against one of the porch stairs. Her eyes numbly tracked the movements of the crows that frequented her yard.

Ember had never thought about befriending the occult wildlife, but it had somehow turned into an opportune accident. One day Ember had thoughtlessly shared half of a tuna salad sandwich with a crow on her porch and then in the blink of an eye she had switched to feeding an entire murder.

At times, it scared Ember how intelligent the birds were with their onyx eyes and sharp reflexes. The feathered friends often seemed to be balancing between one world and the next with their ethereal presence. Of course, such reverent sentiments were easily wiped away after having to clean a generous amount of dropping from the porch. It was a small price to pay for companionship.

"I really stuck my foot in it now. Any suggestions?"

Unsurprisingly, the yard remained eerily quiet aside from the fluttering of wings and pecking of beaks.

Ember tossed out another generous scooping of corn as she mumbled, "Think about it and get back to me."

Chapter 7

Knowing eyes watched Ember's frustrated movements. She reached into the bag and tossed out several vigorous handfuls in the opposite direction of the birds.

Childish.

Her little murder had done nothing wrong. The thought cast the faintest traces of a smile onto her plump lips. It was common for a large group of crows to be called a murder. Ember's little following definitely qualified. The last time that she had bothered to count, there had been around 40 pecky meal-grabbers. Now, that rough estimate seemed to have expanded by at least five or so members.

The sun was slowly making its descent behind the notorious No Man's Land Mountain Ridge. Seemingly impervious to the idea of smooth angles and rounded edges, the mountain pointed sharply into the sky. The uneven and daunting landscape stretched for miles in both directions. Ember always wondered what had possessed the first few settlers to voluntarily trek along such perilous terrain.

If she had been born 200 years ago, Ember knew that she would have waited another two centuries for the invention of planes before even considering such a journey. But then again, desperate people were creative people.

Still, she had no interest in traversing the badlands. No gracias. Estoy bien! The words slipped into the back of her consciousness as the last few rays of sunlight caressed the quickly darkening sky.

A screech struck the air with a resounding high-note. One of the larger birds flapped its massive wings. The other crows momentarily halted their eager scavenging for bits of corn and studiously inspected the yard. A few birds effortlessly leapt into the tolerable night air and disappeared into the distance. The current temperature felt at odds with the typically brisk wintery weather. It was a sure sign that spring was due to make an early appearance.

In Ember's opinion, it was time to thaw the ground. Her crows were now costing her a pretty penny in terms of food. Speaking of pennies, Ember stretched out her legs and noticed a bright object only a few inches away from her toes. Ember leaned down and her fingers found the cool metallic edges of a dime. The dime wasn't all that her house guests had left behind. Ember strode three feet to the right and retrieved the bent medium-sized paperclip. Her sharp-beaked pals were slowly becoming better tippers.

The progress was gradual, but overall unsurprising. For the first month or two, the original birds had simply snubbed all offerings. She had attempted to feed them in vain. It was as if they were on strike. They had simply hid in the trees and watched the ongoings in the yard from above. It wasn't until a few smaller birds had eaten the food and survived that Ember's crows had calculatingly accepted the offerings. After witnessing such intelligence, Ember had eagerly dove into the online bird community. Well, the word eager wasn't exactly right, but the term begrudgingly was also wrong. Perhaps the proper explanation was that Ember had dipped her toe into the bird watching world and learned more about people than she had expected.

    She had openly accepted the task of befriending the standoffish creatures. The birds reminded her of herself, not that she would ever openly make such an admission.

    Perhaps a local neighbor had tried to rid the area of the perceived pests. Some soulless creeps still believed that their land belonged to them more than the wildlife that they stole it from. Furry creatures and avian friends be damned. Ember had a sneaking suspicion that someone had tried to poison the birds in the past. It was the only reason that they would be so cautious about handouts. It was true that for centuries crows had been associated with bad luck and the occult, but that assumption lacked the depth of the true lore. Crows in the sky often indicated a dead animal or corpse was near. It was in their scavenging nature to find and discard the dead. The association between death and crows stuck. After a few hundred years, the lore grew into something that mouth breathing idiots feared. Not that causing fear in the feeble minded was difficult. Ember often found it easy to scare people that knew next to nothing.

However, that easily manipulated fear managed to harm a creature that deserved safety. A place to belong. A home. The thought pulled on Ember's loosely attached heartstrings. She wanted the crows to belong because she knew what it felt like to long for a safe haven that didn't exist.

Sometimes she wondered what she would do if she had wings, but then she remembered that she had a car and still made up excuses to avoid achieving freedom. In some ways, Ember had closed the door to her own cage and contented herself by attempting to care for the little darklings on her property.

Damn it.

She enjoyed the aves more than she cared to admit. Not only because they were intelligent and misunderstood, but also because their simple presence was enough to deter any unwanted visitors. In the last three months, Ember had only needed to deal with one unplanned social interaction. An extremely persistent and hard-selling Butterfly Scout. Ember had bought four boxes of cookies. Partly out of frustration, but mostly out of admiration. Ember had watched the little girl as she had bravely trounced up to the porch. The quaint eggshell colored abode had garnered a reputation that stretched the entire town and then some.

Ember knew the whispers that spread around about a reclusive woman that spent her years well past her prime feeding the bad luck. In a town where there was nothing left to do after 19, but get married and procreate the idea that a woman in her late 20s was alone seemed nearly blasphemous. Between feeding her birds or getting hitched to a mouth breather, spending a few bucks a week on corn seemed like the cheaper option.

To the point, the spunky kiddo had valiantly knocked on Ember's door with a look on her small face that resembled a world leader at a peace conference. The kid had looked so serious and nearly constipated that Ember had nearly laughed. Nearly. She liked the kiddo. The reputation of the home had managed to scare off every adult door-to-door salesperson in the area. On second thought, maybe Ember should have coughed up money for a fifth box of cookies. The memory brought a lazy grin to her face.

With a sigh, Ember unlocked her front door and returned to the sparse, but organized confines of her one-bedroom casita. She dropped the dime and mangled paperclip into a large glass jar near the front door. The contents were crow-selected and steadily growing. It was a fact that often brought a funny sense of satisfaction to Ember's chest. All of her treasures were piled into a Dollar Bin Barrel jar. Ember adored it. She tilted her head to the side as she noticed that the jar was already about halfway full.

Maybe she would need to purchase another jar before St. Patrick's Day. The tentative goal was more than ambitious. Not that it was a goal that she could really sway one way or the other. It wasn't like she was flying around town and searching for shiny shit.

The trainwreck of a day finally hit Ember at full speed. It slammed into her chest and made her hands quiver with anxiety. The impact of the delayed emotions practically kicked her stomach to the floor.

Without thinking, Ember rushed over to the front door and checked that it was locked. For extra measure, she even slid the metallic chain across the stubborn creaky wood. The organic matter rumbled out a loud groan of protest. Was this the first night that Ember had ever elected to latch the top of her door?

Probably.

"You're getting soft, Girl. Ten cuidado."

The warning drifted into the silent room as Ember flitted from one window to the next. She pressed down on each lock at least twice before moving on. The process took less than two minutes given the compact nature of the space. Of course, the expedited task provided Ember with little comfort. What else could she do?

Long-ingrained safety tips and defense techniques flitted through Ember's mind at lightning speed. Tricks and strategies intended to provide comfort and safety to women in the face of danger flowed from her brain like an endless fountain of disturbing knowledge. The amount of information was endless and varied. *Suggestions about never wearing a long ponytail at night to keeping a knife taped to the side of your bed. Have a code word with your best friends to discreetly signal them when you're in trouble. Never take a drink from a stranger at a bar. Avoid drinking from a cup with a wide brim at a restaurant. If you are afraid of getting kidnapped by a rideservice driver, put your fingerprints all over the inside and outside of the car to leave a stronger evidence trail. Leave a massive trail of evidence in the car by plucking out stray hairs and leaving them behind in discreet places like the cracks of the seats. Try to get your attacker's skin under your fingernails to more closely tie them to a potential case.*

    When walking to a car, pretend to use headphones while keeping your keys interlaced between your fingers like miniature knives. Purchase a compact can of pepper spray and make sure it fits every purse. Walk with intention and be aware of your surroundings at all times. Don't check your phone in public because you will appear distracted. Don't listen to music when walking around at night. Don't listen to headphones when taking public transit. Don't listen to music in the car to better check if another driver is following you home. If unsure about being followed, circle the block by making four right hand turns because four right turns will help identify a tail. If being followed, remember police will rarely intervene until given a cause such as a physical altercation. If being followed, drive to the police. Have at least three trusted people know your location at all times. Refrain from sharing your location on social media because it informs potential robbers and kidnappers about your general whereabouts. Make sure to only share your current location with trusted individuals. Don't trust the wrong person with private information because it can be used for exploitation.

All advice pointed to one key theme: Don't live, just survive.

Stifling.

Oppressive.

Counterintuitive.

Pointless.

Distorted.

After several minutes, Ember's list eventually shifted to more relevant content. *Keep a weapon discreetly hidden in multiple areas around the house to increase the odds of survival in a house invasion. Lock your doors and prop a chair underneath the handle to make it more difficult to pry open. Have a phone within easy reach to call for help in case of an intruder. Discreetly put tape on the bottom of all locked windows and doors to know if an intruder recently breached the area.*

Ember didn't have the time or emotional bandwidth to continue thinking about every tip that she had learned and collected over the years. There were too many. Better yet, why did she even need to know so many? Why did every woman that Ember knew manage to tell her a new bit of advice? Why was it that every woman in Ember's life shared and exchanged survival tactics as if they were baking recipes? Why did the inevitable conversation come up so often and so frequently about survival? If women were being so brutally and obviously hunted in the states, why did no one care?

Simple.

It was an extremely successful blame game. The blame was always placed on the wrong party. A real damned if you do and damned if you don't situation for every woman living in the states. It was a culture that emphasized shame. Shame imposed on the victim to the point that trading survival tactics while waiting in line at the public restroom seemed like a standard practice.

Ember couldn't count the number of women in her life and within her immediate circle that had been hurt. The number kept growing.

Faces twisted and turned in agony. It was always the same bottomless, distant look. It was as if the Earth had swallowed something whole and then insisted that the piece had never existed in the first place.

A whispered problem. A silent inconvenience. Something to be given the occasional spotlight instead of an actual stage.

Ember stewed in her escalating anger. The fear had shifted into emboldened rage. The hopelessness left her bones as a call to action burned deep within her veins.

A compulsion.

She padded into her pint-sized kitchen and sighed. Where was it? Where the hell was it? Ember opened a cabinet and riffled through the burnt pots and pans. Zilch. A second cabinet proved more successful. Bingo.

An unopened bottle of red wine was calling Ember's name. She smacked the bottle onto the counter and cursed at the harsh impact. Luckily, the cheap bottle refused to shatter. Ember clapped her hands together in victory. Now, where was the corkscrew?

Ember was just about to embark on a feral recon mission when she noticed that the bottle was a twist cap. That made more sense. Let the games begin.

One full and very generous pour later, Ember was feeling motivated. Her body hummed with energy as her mind swirled with faces. Friends. Family. Work associates.

No.

Ember opted for the bottle once she drained the contents of her glass. She brought her laptop and recording material to the center of her threadbare rug. She clumsily curled her legs underneath her body as she took another long swig from the bottle.

Ember's slightly hazy vision was blurred with a combination of fury and liquor. Her limbs thrummed with rage as she pounded her index finger against the red record button.

"I'm coming for you, Asshole."

Oh, well. She'd edit out the beginning of the episode. If she remembered.

Chapter 8

The bed felt firmer than Ember remembered as it pressed into her clammy skin. Why had she decided to purchase a bargain value mattress? That's right, because it had been the only one in her price range. The price range being somewhere between dirt poor and broke. With a notable amount of effort, Ember opened her eyes.

That couldn't be right. Ember furiously rubbed her eyes with the back of her palm in an attempt to clear her vision. She had to be dreaming.

The insistent pain that blossomed just behind her eyes hinted at an alternative solution. Ember looked to her right and noticed an opened bottle tilted to the side, completely empty. Not a drop of liquid spilled onto the laminated floor. Did she do that?

Ember groaned, "I haven't done that since high school."

The blank computer screen was positioned one telling, inebriated breath away from the bottle. The dark screen caught Ember's attention. She almost physically shuddered at the thought of checking her own browser history. Almost. Ember quickly tapped on the track pad. The screen dutifully blazed to life. The image displayed by the hundreds of luminous pixels threatened to rob Ember of all of the remaining vigor in her body.

    That was the last time that she was drinking wine. Bargain screw cap wine, at least.

Chapter 9

The number bordered on asinine. Incomprehensible. Better yet, impossible. How could she possibly have gained 30,000 followers on her podcast homepage overnight? Was this some kind of sick joke? Had Mrs. Van Scorn suddenly enlisted the help of a tech-savvy teen to torture her? The option didn't seem very likely. However, stranger things have happened. For example, an unknown killer committing a crime down to the last detail, exactly how Ember had described it.

The episode.

Memories from the night before competed for attention as they formed a disjointed movie in the back of Ember's mind. Her index finger shakily scrolled to her podcast's episode section. An unfamiliar episode was outlined in green. The 35-minute episode was marked as new. The symbols on the right-hand side of the screen indicated that it currently had 30,000 listens and counting. The number crawled up to 30,006 as Ember stared, completely flabbergasted at the screen.

A loud trill played through the air. Ember was willing to bet all of her remaining bank account that she knew exactly who was calling.

She accepted the call, "Ms. Lopez, it's Detective Godford."

Before Detective Godford could continue, Ember plowed over, "I know. Let me put on pants before you cart me away."

Chapter 10

Maybe this wasn't Ember's week. The intrusive thought popped into her head as she begrudgingly returned to the police station. Ember was curious about the likelihood that she was going to end up in jail for the obstruction of justice. Given the climbing number of listeners on her two most recent podcast episodes, the option seemed extremely high.

However, Ember no longer cared. Some sick freak was making it a game to harm women for sport. It wasn't exactly her little episodes that had invited the violence. The episodes were simply a thinly-veiled excuse. A horrible, twisted weak excuse to commit atrocities.

A wave of unease washed down the back of Ember's spine as every set of eyes in the department looked up at her arrival. She tried her best to ignore the heavy gazes. Many of the familiar faces appeared permanently etched with disgust.

Fair enough.

Ember already knew that even if she wasn't guilty of committing murder, the town would still unofficially link her name to the horrendous acts. Indirectly, it would be her fault. The illogical line of thought was that she was at least guilty of something. It didn't matter that she couldn't be put on trial for such a sentiment. The court of public opinion had already ruled against her favor. The court had consistently ruled against her since the first day that her tanned butt had driven into town.

"Please step into my office, Ms. Lopez."

"Sure," Ember did her best to hide her surprise. Since when did Detective Godford have an actual office at the station? Hadn't he simply been brought in from a few towns over to solve the case?

Ember entered the sparsely decorated room and noticed the whiteboard that stretched from one wall to another. Faint traces of the previous project ghosted the erasable surface. It was too faint to properly discern words, but the smudges vaguely resembled letters. After a cursory inspection, Ember realized that it was a makeshift office. It was the general meeting room where officers likely congregated for weekly briefings. Not that there was ever any pressing news.

Until now.

Detective Godford indicated with the tilt of his head that Ember could sit down in the chair opposite the lengthy meeting room desk. The relaxed setting was a stark change in pace from the previously cold steel seat and immovable table. In comparison, the current room looked like the lap of luxury.

A small frown gave Ember's facial features a pensive look. The detective hunkered down into his seat and folded his arms across his broad chest. His knee easily knocked against the side of the low table as he brought his chair closer to the center of the room. A power play.

Ember tried her best to refrain from rolling her eyes. It was obvious that she was in enough trouble already. What else was she in for? Besides a very poorly created and extremely drunk podcast episode. Heat crawled up the sides of Ember's neck as she tried her best to focus on the conversation. Not that the detective was currently saying much of anything. He was simply silently observing Ember.

Eventually, he asked, "How close were you to Ms. Stanley?"

"What?"

"If you had to guess, how often did you speak to Ms. Stanley during the week?"

The questions caught Ember by surprise as she opened and closed her mouth as if to chew over every syllable. She hadn't exactly gone out her way to speak to the woman, but Ms. Stanley had always been amicable.

"We were neighbors when I first moved in. She left for a more affluent corner of town about a month later. It's a small town, but she's one of the kinder women. I don't know what happened, but she definitely did not kill anyone. The woman gets visibly ill just at the mention of taxidermied animals or road kill. She's just not up for this type of thing."

"You just referred to murder as this type of thing. That's very casual of you," Detective Godford arched an infuriating eyebrow as if daring Ember to keep going.

Of course, Ember had no self-preservation so she simply kept digging deeper. She replied, "The woman is unmarried and in her late 30s, but everybody in town adores her. It's not so unheard of for people to snap, but not Ms. Stanley. She would probably bring you flowers if you ever yelled at her."

The last sentence wasn't a guess. Ember had once snapped at Ms. Stanley over a stupid dispute near the produce aisle. The next morning, Ms. Stanley had brought two carrier mugs of coffee to the supermarket as an apology for the squabble that Ember had started. It was an apology that in all fairness, Ember should have made. Not the other way around.

"Did you hear me?"

What?"

"Ms. Stanley was murdered."

Chapter 11

Another woman was gone. She had been forcefully shoved off the mortal coil before her time.

Vivith Stanley had made a life for herself as a school teacher. She had steadily ascended the ranks and reached the role of Vice Principal at Sunnybrooks Elementary. All of her work was now left unfinished. Her life was like a book that had the majority of its pages torn from existence.

Painfully incomplete.

Ember gripped the armrest. The coolness of the metal helped to anchor her to the moment. How many women were going to die before this psychopath was arrested? Why was this happening?

She hesitated to ask the most obvious question. The words seemed to be illuminated on a neon sign, but Ember shied away from repeating them out loud. Deep breath. Steady. Respirar.

Ember licked her lower lip as she struggled to ask, "Did Vivith pass quickly?"

The unsaid question remained. However, Ember hoped that she would be able to read between the lines of Detective Godford's response.

"She didn't suffer. She passed from hypothermia. Her body simply shut down before anything happened. I can't tell you the details."

Godford knew exactly what Ember had been too afraid to ask. Luckily, he had spared her the discomfort of crawling to the final task. She needed to know if Vivith had suffered but had feared directly asking the question. Detective Godford had given her a small consolation in the face of unending misery.

The floor appeared so much more interesting than usual. Ember tapped the floor with her shoes and noticed how the fake wood gleamed beneath her feet. It had obviously seen the weight of many people given the rips and knicks in the tarnished surface.

"When?"

"I can't disclose further information."

"A rough estimate."

"Why does it matter so much?"

Ember ran her tongue along the grooves of her teeth. She slowly looked up and realized that Godford's features lacked their usual smug quality. Great. He was serious. A second round of understanding rammed into the first and Ember groaned.

Detective Godford hadn't heard about her newest podcast tirade. Ember hadn't clicked on it to listen, but she could only guess what her wine-addled brain had said.

"You're going to toss me in jail. For the record, I don't eat meat and would prefer a cellmate that doesn't smell like feet or cheese. I once had a roommate with smelly feet and it was the worst. Her name was Tiffany and I hated that demon."

"I have no idea what you're talking about."

The door to the office creaked open as a burly officer entered the room with a decade-old laptop in tow. Ember easily noticed her podcast logo brightly illuminated on the screen. Her annoying smile seemed to taunt her about the current and completely avoidable situation that she had managed to get herself into. It was a stupid photo. A dumbass face. Ember supposed it was a fitting look for the situation.

"You'll want to hear this," The newcomer looked at Detective Godford and then pressed play as he chomped into a chocolate sprinkled donut. Sprinkles landed all over the floor and Detective Godford gave a strangled cry. It was so faint that Ember was sure that the sprinkled-covered genius near the door hadn't heard it.

A smug sense of satisfaction crept into Ember's chest. She enjoyed watching Detective Godford's momentary discomfort. Good. Mr. Sprinkles could drop a few more of the sugary pieces of edible confetti on the ground. It wasn't going to kill anyone. Someone else already had that position covered.

The screen blared to life as the officer placed the whirring laptop onto the extremely large table and selected the newest episode. A spiral appeared on the screen. It whirled in a circular pattern that threatened to drive Ember insane with impatience.

She tapped her foot. The sprinkle lover turned to her and shrugged apologetically, "Budget cuts."

Ember returned the same amount of effort by responding with a noncommittal grunt. Suddenly, her voice slurred from the speakers, "I'm coming for you, Asshole."

Immediately, Ember felt a headache coming on as she sat in silence, completely mortified by her newest episode. It was an episode, alright. Her emotions were so clear that Ember felt that same spark of fury return. She frowned at the injustice of the entire situation.

She was slightly ashamed that anyone that knew her would be able to notice the drunken lilt to her tone. She tended to have a much higher pitched voice after a few drinks, but mercifully it wasn't as telling as she had imagined. The newest podcast episode was a few steps away from a trainwreck.

Once the episode ended, Detective Godford leaned all that way back in his chair. Usually, he enjoyed giving Ember a rough time. His sudden contemplative silence made Ember uneasy. What was going on in that unreasonably attractive and stubborn head of his?

Officer Sprinkles exited the tab as an advertisement for kitten adoptions appeared on his screen. The kittens were bright white and fluffy beyond belief. The officer noticed Ember's line of sight and swiftly slammed the laptop shut as he blustered, "For my daughter."

"You don't have a daughter, Matt," Detective Godford quipped as he kept his gaze fixed on a section of the ceiling that appeared to have accumulated several years worth of water damage.

"Maybe I just don't know about her yet. College was wild." With that lame reply, Matt scrambled out of the room. He was clearly unable to accept the beauty in the softer side of life.

Detective Godford carefully turned his attention back to Ember as he questioned, "Did you catch how many listens that episode had?"

"Not right now, but this morning there were a few."

"Over 100,000 listens and climbing."

Detective Godford's voice sounded too calm. He appeared deceptively collected as his arms remained casually folded over his broad chest. The only indication that he was marginally displeased was the fact that his eyebrows were knit together more tightly than the rope of a fisherman's net.

"You've really done it now, Ember."

"I still mean every word."

"You just put the largest target on your back."

"I intended to erase the part at the beginning, but I forgot," Ember scrunched up her face and slapped the bottom of her palm down on the table in frustration.

A rumbling from the back of Detective Godford's throat caught Ember by surprise. At first, she thought that he was choking until the sound in the back of his throat gathered momentum and turned into a booming laugh.

"That part was the tamest section out of the entire episode. I am willing to bet my entire career that the killer already listened to this new development. Likely, the killer was one of your very first listeners."

"I'm no longer the main suspect?"

Ember narrowed her eyes and leaned across the table. She trusted this man as far as she could throw him. She doubted that she could even lift him an inch from the ground given their notable size and weight differences. Ember was more likely to throw her back out trying to lift him than actually making any progress.

"Right. At the moment, you're not a suspect. Now you are very likely to be the next victim if not the last victim on the killer's list."

"What?"

"You've just signed yourself up for constant surveillance."

Ember stood from her chair and tossed her hands up in disbelief, "No way! It was one tiny dig."

"You insulted a serial killer. Do you think a psychopath cares about the size of the insult? It's obvious that the killer has an unusual interest in you. The first murder was modeled after your podcast."

Ember was about to object, but Detective Godford beat her to it as he added, "You're stuck with me or you get to spend another night in jail. I have more than enough evidence to hold you for contempt. I told you to leave the podcast alone. Instead, you decided the best option was to ignore my advice. Congratulations. Why don't you just pour gasoline all over your body before running into a dry forest and lighting a match? It would save both of us time."

"That's a vivid description. Did you ever think of becoming an author or did you always know that you'd have a better time harassing people in real life?"

A vein near the side of Detective Godford's forehead pulsed with irritation. Perhaps Ember had actually hit a nerve. Instead of continuing the squabble, he drawled, "The sooner that you realize that we are on the same team, the better off you will be."

"So you say," Ember placed her hands on the table and pushed back. She tilted her chair and allowed it to momentarily balance on its back legs before permitting it to clatter back to the ground. The momentary weightlessness mimicked the disturbing sensation blossoming in the center of Ember's chest. She wanted to reach inside of her body and rip out the blossoming fear. Cut out the growing sense of helplessness that appeared to attack her balance and catapulted her into an emotional state of limbo. She was stuck somewhere between the sky and the ground. Just waiting for the inevitable impact. The front legs of the low-budget chair smacked into the ground.

"How do you feel about jail?"

The sardonic smirk that ghosted along Detective Godford's face made Ember's decision only that much more difficult to verbalize. Not that it really mattered. The detective's lips imperceptibly crooked into a smile. His knowing facial expression made Ember wish that she had a chancla. Just one swat to his smug face. Just one whack and then she'd agree to staying the night in jail. Unfortunately, the room appeared to be devoid of slippers.

Her options appeared less than attractive. What was she going to do? Ember nibbled on her lower lip as she anxiously tried to find an alternative. Unfortunately, supervision did sound like a reasonable option. Not that Ember had any intention of saying that out loud. Instead she sighed, "Fine. Only because I don't want a cellmate with stinky feet."

Chapter 12

"Is this usually how you usually spend your mornings?"

"No, usually I spend the beginning of my morning reorganizing soup cans and bargaining with middle schoolers to put back the bikini clad cutout beer model near the back of the mart. I hate that damn life-size cutout. My boss used to dock my pay every time it ended up stolen."

Godford snorted as he took a generous sip of coffee and stared at the lake. A low layer of fog rolled over the surrounding uneven mounds of leaves and caressed the surface of the dark swirling water. Ember had left the police department. She had grabbed a coffee before deciding to take a detour at the lake. The wet wooden park bench dampened the back of Ember's jeans, but she didn't care. It was nice to get some fresh air. The area would likely be empty for a few more hours. Dog walkers and joggers typically waited until the morning fog receded before making an appearance.

"How did you convince the kids not to steal the cardboard cutout?"

"I didn't."

"I don't follow."

"I gave the ringleader strict instructions to wait ten minutes after the end of my shift to take it. Not like anyone else working in the store would get their pay docked."

"Why would the rules only apply to you? Isn't that pretty defeatist to believe that the entire system is out to get you?"

"You've clearly got it all twisted around. The rule was designed to specifically apply to me. I'm not Mr. Bleeker's blood."

"That's a twisted type of logic."

"It's small town logic. The kids now take the cutout about twice a month, but Bleeker always has a few spares shoved into the store room. It's become a real exciting challenge for the kids to try and steal it before Bleeker catches them and calls their parents."

"Why aren't you stacking soup cans today?"

Damn. Ember had hoped that telling Godford the funny story would distract him from asking questions. Apparently, the little conversation-piece had failed. Godford saw the details when most people only saw the big picture. The realization sent fresh waves of unease into Ember's belly. She took a deep sip of her sludge-like coffee and sighed. It was going to be difficult to get him off her back.

"I proactively resigned. It's not easy to keep a job when you're accused of being a murderer."

"Ember, you were never accused of a crime."

"You brought me in for questioning and had every reason to believe that I committed the murder. Now, you can only prove that I didn't actually execute the second murder, but my alibi is still too weak to prove my innocence. We both know that. Which means I need to solve the murder or the killer needs to become real sloppy real fast. Every pair of eyes in town is still looking in my direction. As if they needed another reason."

Ember grumbled as she looked down at her tanned skin that had at one time been a darker shade of bronze. Her limited time outside had managed to make it lighter. A color that was simultaneously too dark and yet also several shades too light.

If Detective Godford understood the brooding undertone behind Ember's words then he was polite enough not to pick at it. Perhaps he wasn't the vulture that he had so adamantly portrayed. In the station, he had picked at Ember's every word.

"What's your first name?"

"My first name?"

"This isn't a game of telephone. Yes, you know my name and probably everything about me. I'm sure there is a manila file somewhere with all of my details in it and I bet that you already read over all of the content. The least I should be able to know is your name."

Godford stretched out his long legs as he readjusted his position on the bench. His frame was too large for the skimpy slats of wood.

"First off, your information isn't in a manila folder."

Ember arched an incredulous eyebrow as she crossed her arms over her chest in disbelief.

Detective Godford held out his palms in mock surrender as he continued, "Your information is in an online portfolio. The department is old school, but it's just modern enough to use computer documents with a bullshit user interface. Now to get to the second point, I don't owe you my name. You're a person of interest in a murder investigation. My last name should be more than enough."

Ember was about to roll her eyes, but Detective Godford suddenly relented, "It's Ray."

"I'd say it's nice to meet you, but I really haven't enjoyed the last 48 hours."

"That's fair. What's that across the water?"

The heavy fog was dissipating. Across the stagnant water, an imposing building was slowly becoming visible. Its red brick exterior sharply contrasted the dark browns of the sparse tree branches that appeared to perfectly frame the imposing structure.

"That's the hospital and next door is the cemetary."

"I can't tell if that's genius or nefarious city planning."

"I lean towards the latter. The planner of that design should have been fired. No one needs a visual reminder of where we all end up when they're fighting to stay. Makes it all a little too defeatist."

"Interesting."

"What?"

"Nothing. I just didn't expect the owner of a true crime podcast to feel so passionately about motivating the human spirit. Makes you a wild card."

Ember pursed her lips together and then opened them with a smack as she mumbled, "Maybe I am."

Ray remained quiet as he regarded her from the corner of his eyes. Ember wasn't exactly sure what he was thinking, but she didn't exactly care. People were brought into existence every day and the only thing that really mattered was the small blip between life and death. The only part of the circle that people had been able to see for thousands of years. It seemed silly to fear the next phase, but that didn't mean that Ember didn't burn with an eternal fury at the knowledge that a killer was skulking around town and extinguishing young promising lives before their time. The act was pure veil.

Worried about the darkness surrounding her derailing train of thought, Ember took a long sip from her coffee. The last sip was bitter as the coffee grounds poured between her teeth. Ember swallowed the mud in two gulps.

The gray tombstones appeared to float above a receding layer of fog. The weather made it look as if the concrete slabs were moving through the River Nyx. A river that eventually everyone traveled, but many found too soon.

Ember narrowed her eyes at the sight as the cold chill in the air nipped against her cheeks. The temperamental fog had somehow managed to weave around the bench. Never touching her ankles.

Chapter 13

Leaves scrunched with every step of Ember's unhurried journey. Her shoulders bristled with irritation. The slow ten minute walk wasn't enough time for Ember to gather her nerves. She had simply precariously tied a few strands of courage together and hoped that would suffice.

A little gumption was better than none. Besides, she needed to drive to her mailbox. The mailbox was just on the outskirts of town in the sleepy older version of the post office that was now located on Main Street. With only a handful of rented boxes, Ember preferred the tiny shop to the commotion and curiosity often found closer to the hub of town. For the journey, she needed to pick up her car from the mart parking lot. The unforeseen events of the morning had derailed her timeline. Her lips pulled into a thin line once the storefront finally came into focus.

"I thought that you quit?"

"I did."

"Why are we here?"

Ray swiveled his head around the perimeter and then turned his attention to the mart doors. A handful of people loitered around the first few rows of parking spots.

Ember felt relieved. She realized that she had parked in the back of the parking lot. Maybe she had a chance at sliding into her little car and speeding away before anyone from the store could say a damn word. It was worth a shot.

"Keep up. We're heading to my car."

"You left it here overnight?"

"I hadn't been in the mood to drive."

The wide open spots churned Ember's stomach with dread. The vast, unprotected parking lot allowed any person inside of the store to see her skulking form. So much for subtlety. Ember increased her pace. She listened as a markedly heavy set of footsteps struggled to keep up. A small smile momentarily played near the edges of Ember's lips. She felt Ray's presence a few inches behind her back. She appreciated that he was committed to getting her car out of the lot as quickly as possible.

Ember reached into her pocket and unlocked her car doors. A prompt swishing sound informed Ember that the passenger side door had been disarmed. She sped around the car and opened the passenger door.

"The driver's door is jammed."

"Oh," Ray's one-syllable response held no malice. In fact, Ember swore that she detected the faintest traces of amusement as she shimmied over the console and plopped into the driver's seat.

"What are you looking at? Get in the car."

"Look who came crawling back." Mr. Bleeker's condescending tone had Ember gripping the steering wheel for dear life.

Ray was still outside of the car as Mr. Bleeker sidled over to the vehicle with an overly confident smile. He placed a hand on the roof of Ember's vehicle and leaned down so that his breath created small patches of condensation against the dirty driver's side window.

"Knew you needed a job. Women always come back, right?"

Mr. Bleeker leaned up and offered the comment as a form of greeting to Ray. It was obvious that the stout spineless man was desperately trying to impress Ray.

Ray's gaze grew cool. He stood taller and subtly blocked the open passenger door with his figure. Not that it particularly mattered given that Mr. Bleeker was moments away from dripping slobber all over Ember's driver side window. Ray looked down his nose at Mr. Bleeker. The look conveyed that the tiny man was less valuable than the mud still caked on the bottom of Ray's shoes.

Insignificant and troublesome.

The response unsettled Mr. Bleeker and he slowly slid his hands off the roof of Ember's car. He narrowed his gaze as he stumbled for his next words.

Not that Ember intended to wait around and find out what horrible string of words he could come up with next.

She shoved her key into the ignition. The dashboard beeped to life as several alerts illuminated the panel. The check engine light coupled with the brake light. Ember didn't bother to read what the other two lights meant. At the end of the day, they all signaled the same thing, money.

"I'm just getting my car," Ember swallowed the ball of embarrassment that bubbled in the back of her throat. She knew that Mr. Bleeker was intentionally goading her by trying to degrade her in front of Ray. He wanted to make Ember pay for walking out on him and for putting him in his place. Ember's angry reaction to the injustice was only reasonable, but Mr. Bleeker obviously did not share such sentiments.

Ray crouched into the car. His knees tapped against the dashboard as he closed the door. He was much too large for the compact vehicle, but he didn't complain. Instead, he swiftly buckled his seat belt.

As soon as Ember heard the metallic click, she took the car out of park and lightly revved the engine. Mr. Bleeker took a step back as an angry shade of red crawled up the base of his pudgy neck. Ember momentarily wondered if his brightly colored cheeks were a result of fury or embarrassment. Likely it was a combination of both.

Mr. Bleeker's belly shook as he rapidly waved his hands above his head and tried to walk to the front of Ember's car.

"Hitting someone with my car is murder."

"I might make an exception in this case," Ray grumbled as he narrowed his eyes at Mr. Bleeker.

For once, it felt nice to have another person on her team. She enjoyed having someone back her up. Even if it was subtle.

"Promise to bail me out?"

"Absolutely."

Ember laughed as she turned out of the parking lot. The sound came from deep in her chest and bubbled from her lips. She turned right and then headed onto the road. The sudden shift in her mood caught her by surprise. Ray mumbled something under his breath.

"What?"

Ember quickly glanced at Ray as she examined his face.

Ray coughed, "Nothing. Where are we going next?"

Ember shrugged, "My place. Maybe you'll get to know my pets."

"How many do you have?"

"I lost count around 15. I'm not really sure since they come and go as they please."

Ray groaned, "A crazy cat lady that runs a murder podcast. That's great."

Ember was having so much fun that she didn't bother correcting him.

"I prefer the term cat connoisseur."

A smile threatened to ruin Ember's fib. She clamped down on her bottom lip and avoided looking in Ray's direction. Her poker face would give her little fun away. Instead, she waved a finger in Ray's direction, but kept her eyes on the road as she teased, "Don't judge a book by its cover."

Chapter 14

"Your house doesn't smell like you have 15 cats."

"You don't miss a beat."

Ember locked the front door and then patted Ray's back in a similar fashion to a subtly disappointed parent. She shimmied around his massive form and placed her car keys in the small bowl on the kitchen counter.

The compact single bedroom house was a small squeeze for one person. Ember was sure that two people in such close quarters were bound to feel like a circus.

"You don't have cats."

Ray's deadpanned statement contrasted with his indignant expression as he walked deeper into the living room. He looked out of place near the tan sofa and bundled yoga mat. It was a mat that Ember might have used twice since the start of the year. Two moments when she thought that she would start a healthier new year. Now, she just wanted to survive.

"No, but I do have animals that depend on me."

"Don't tell me, you upgraded from cats to rats," Ray cautiously scanned the majority of the house with one long glance. The confined space made it nearly possible to see the entire layout. Only the bathroom and bedroom were hidden from view.

"I need to use your restroom before I'm sacrificed to the rodents."

"Sure. Go into the bedroom and it's the door on the right."

Ember opened the cabinet where she stored the majority of the food supply for her feathered friends. She pulled out a fresh bag of corn and plucked a small baggie of assorted seeds. The heavy bag of corn tilted to the side and Ember grumbled in protest as she struggled to keep it upright. The weight wasn't evenly distributed so it was listing to the side. The damn 40 pound bag was threatening to knock her over.

"Let me," Ray returned to the kitchen and gripped the bag of corn with one hand.

Ember sighed in relief, "Thanks."

"Where do you want this?"

"Follow me. We're running late."

"Why does it matter if we're late?"

Ember rolled her eyes. It was a pointless gesture given that Ray couldn't see it from his position following her lead. She decided to make an effort to be cordial and explained, "They have an excellent sense of time. If I leave then they will throw a protest."

"So you feed the neighborhood bullies pieces of corn and seeds to keep them from knocking down your house?"

"Kinda. I feed them and make sure to do it on time. If I'm more than 10 minutes late then someone gets the bright idea to break my roof."

Ember paused and decided to clarify. She didn't want to sound overdramatic, "Not the entire roof. They will usually toss down a few shingles, but that does add up and I don't like the idea of needing to replace any part of the roof before my lease is up."

"I don't know if I want to meet your pets." Ray tightened his grip on the bag.

Ember opened the front door to several dark-feathered tyrants crowing in protest. She snuck a subtle glance in Ray's direction. Part of her wanted to know how he would react. Better yet, Ember wanted to see if the crows would interpret him as a threat. The birds seemed to have an acute understanding of people. It was almost otherworldly how impressive the intelligent brooding bunch could be.

She pointed at a spot on the floor and Ray unceremoniously lowered the bag. It plopped to the floor and the impact elicited a lazy groan from the wood. The porch was old and often cried when anything heavier than a crow dared to step foot. It was like an old-fashioned alarm that didn't have an off switch.

One of the larger birds swooped down from the sky and landed only a few feet away from Ember's toes. He stretched out his wings as he hopped around on the porch as he crowed in indignation.

"I'm here, Brutus. Calm down," Ember opened the new bag of corn and tossed a handful into the yard. She typically refrained from feeding the crows from her stairs because their speckled defecation was a constant issue. She loved the little difficult birds, but passionately despised their parting gifts.

Brutus tossed his head back and released a nearly furious caw. Obviously, he was distraught at the idea of not being fed.

"You are such a baby," Ember grabbed a generous amount of seed and held out her palm.

Brutus swiftly accepted her offer. He hopped along the wooden boards and then pecked a few times at Ember's hand. In less than a few seconds, Ember's hand was empty.

"He tends to be a bit greedier than the rest when I'm late. I think he takes it personally."

"I would take it personally too if that meant getting fed extra."

Ember tilted one of her shoulders in a half-shrug as she tossed another handful of corn into the center of her yard. She didn't have much interest in talking and luckily Ray seemed to agree. He kept silent and watched Ember from the back of the porch.

Crows landed in the yard from all different directions. Some swooped from the highest point of the surrounding trees while others flew low to the ground like military bomber planes before deftly landing.

Ray walked closer to Ember as his jaw slackened in amazement. The yard was now a mixture of dull green grass and vibrant black spots. Crows mulled around the yard and Ember decided to let Ray try. She walked over to the bag of corn and carefully nudged it with her foot in Ray's direction.

He grabbed about half a palmful of corn and then looked around the yard. Ray spent a few minutes getting the lay of the land before tossing the corn to the right. A few of the younger birds often congregated closer to the back. They tended to stay away from the front where the older and more dominant individuals were known to get into the occasional scuffle.

Ember narrowed her eyes, "Why did you throw it over there?"

"Looked like they could use it."

Instead of replying, Ember simply made a noise in the back of her throat. She settled into a comfortable position on the unforgiving stairs. Ray squatted down to her left and the duo intently observed the yard. A light breeze swept Ember's dark hair to the side. The comfortable silence was sporadically broken by the occasional caw and impatient fluttering of wings.

After a few minutes, the sky began to darken. The birds retreated back to their nightly routines and Ember lifted her arms above her head to stretch. The stress from the past few days felt like a constant weight upon her shoulders, but the brief moments spent with her birds somehow managed to lessen the strain.

"I hate to say this, but I like your friends a lot more than most people."

Ember jumped. Ray had been so silent that Ember had momentarily forgotten about him. She tilted her head up so that she could catch Ray's relaxed gaze.

"You're the first person I've let feed them. They're important to me."

The words were an understatement. Ember adored her mini raptors. They somehow made even the darkest day a bit brighter.

"Thank you. It's very quiet so far out of town. The crows are the only real noise for miles."

A teasing smile lifted Ember's mouth into a crooked grin, "It's my ranchito on a budget."

"What does that mean?"

"My little ranch. I grew up a city girl, but the idea of having a closer connection to nature was undeniably attractive. The tradcoff for leaving the city is that salt and pepper are the only main condiments for miles."

Ember's nose wrinkled as she mulled over her last sentence. She missed the food from her childhood. The flavorful meats and the smell of fresh street vendor tacos after a late night concert. Food that smelled of home and tasted like decades of loving abuelas.

"Do you miss the city?"

"Parts of it. I miss the food and the noise. Not the excessive car honking, but just enough sound to know that something 's happening in the background. I barely slept the first few months that I lived here. The quiet felt unnatural. I couldn't hear all of the wildlife that everyone talks about when they move out of the city. It was just dead silence."

Ray turned his attention back to the front of the yard as his eyebrows scrunched together in thought. He idly patted the rickety wood with his knuckles and created a dull rolling rhythm.

"That doesn't make any sense. I'm just 20 minutes up the interstate and I can barely sleep during the summer because of the nocturnal concert that likes to play outside of my windows until the break of dawn. The wildlife here should be just as noisy."

"A lot of things aren't making sense," Ember sighed as the deeper meaning behind her words deflated the mood like a child letting out all of the air out of a balloon. Her shoulders subtly slumped in defeat. How had she gotten into this mess? A large part of her knew that it was because she had decided to open her damn chatty mouth. However, a larger part of her resented that logic. Why was she responsible for the unhinged acts of a killer? Was it worse to be the killer or the unwitting instigator? At the end of the day, did it really matter? Were they both considered culprits? Were both parties equally guilty?

A shiver slithered down Ember's spine as she tried to wrestle with a faceless monster. She tried to grapple against a force that was slowly encircling her and constricting around her throat.

"Do you like pizza?"

"What?"

"Pizza. An Americanized delicacy. Often comes from a chain that offers unreasonable discounts for massive quantities of cheesy goodness."

Ember's lip twitched at Ray's forced injection of levity. She knew that he was purposely trying to lift the gloom hanging in the air. It was a kind gesture. Ember stood from her seated position and stretched as she teased, "Pizza works. Any preference?"

"Meat and cheese. I'm a simple man."

"Nothing wrong with simple. I'll take my half with vegetables."

"Only vegetables?"

"I still plan to have cheese and tomato sauce as the base."

Ray didn't say anything for a moment. Instead, he kept his tone deceptively impassive as he offered, "How about we each get our own pizza?"

"How diplomatic of you. Has anyone ever taught you that sharing is caring? Besides, I just quit my job because someone managed to make me a top person of interest in a string of grisly murders. I don't have the funds to purchase an entire pizza on my own. Even with all of the coupons and discounts."

Ember arched a haughty eyebrow as if daring Ray to reply. She had no interest in spending more money than necessary. Especially now that she needed to be extra careful with her spending habits. It wasn't like she had much in the way of savings. Ember knew that she was in trouble if she couldn't find a job before her next rent payment was due. The worries were mounting, but Ember decided to shove them all to the back of her mind. They would need to stay tucked away, at least for now.

"You win, but let's at least order a large pizza. Otherwise I'll be tempted to dig into the bag of corn for a late night snack. Speaking of corn."

Ray's voice trailed off as he swiftly hefted the bag of corn over his head. He called, "Where would you like this?"

"In the large cabinet under the kitchen sink," Ember opened the front door and allowed Ray to enter first. Before Ember went inside, a faint twinkle caught her attention. She walked over to the farthest end of the porch and retrieved a dirty dime. It was covered in mud, but it still managed to shimmer in the light. She plucked the kind gift from the ground and brought it inside. The trinket was a present that she had almost left outside. Ember didn't want her little friends to think that she was ungrateful.

    Even though she was sure that they wouldn't hear, Ember murmured, "Thank you," as she locked the front door.

Chapter 15

"Do you want to keep your leftovers in a container?"

"You say the word leftovers like it's a bad thing."

"It's only bad because there isn't a speck of meat on one of those slices."

"Not true. One of your sausages cooked into the corner of one of my slices. I barely complained."

"Barely? You made me pick it off with a fork. Which makes no sense because we were eating pizza with our hands. So why did I need a fork to pick off one tiny speck of spicy meat?"

"I don't know where you've been. It's just smart to be extra careful."

Ray snorted, "So now you want to be careful. I'm going to pretend that in some world that isn't an insult."

"Smart man," Ember teased as she packed away her remaining slices of pizza. Ray had managed to finish all of his in about the span of one sneeze. He ate as if it was his last meal on Earth. A small part of Ember was relieved that they had agreed to split the large. In retrospect, maybe the extra large size would have been better.

"Okay, it was great having you over. What time do you plan to come back tomorrow?"

Ember placed a hand on her hip as she turned away from the sink to face Ray. She tapped a hand against her counter in an expectant manner.

A slow smile crept along Ray's features as he leaned against the counter. He folded his arms across his chest and teased, "I'm not going anywhere. Either I stay the night or I can call someone else from the department to take this shift. It's up to you."

"What are you saying?"

"You know exactly what I'm saying. You just really wish that it was a misunderstanding."

Ember was momentarily glad that they hadn't ordered the extra large. Why was he smiling like that? She struggled to control her bubbling frustration as she ground out, "So I will have the extreme pleasure of having you skulk around my house all night or switch you out for an even more uncertain stranger?"

"You catch on fast."

Ember refused to validate Ray's nonsense with an answer. Instead, she momentarily disappeared from sight. She begrudgingly opened her sparsely stocked linen closet and pulled out a spare blanket and pillow case. Ember handed the items to Ray and then called over her shoulder, "I'm taking a shower."

"Take your time."

"That's the plan."

With any luck, Ember would be able to scrub away the last traces of her horrible day. Of course, the problem with removing dirt was that it had a way of coming back. Especially right after a thorough wash.

Chapter 16

Ember wiped away the condensation that kissed the bathroom mirror with the back of her hand. The dampness clung to her skin as she took the first real look at her face since chaos had descended into her life.

Deep circles clung beneath her eyes and the dark shadows appeared to pull her face downward. She was the image of permanent exhaustion. Her typically bright hair appeared dull, but Ember tried to reason that it was still drenched from the shower. She stepped over the wide grate located near the bottom of the bathroom floor. The heat pushed through the grate; Ember appreciated the warmth even if the actual grate that eventually led to the outside of her house was unsightly.

"Fine, so I won't win a beauty pageant at the moment."

She tossed on a fresh change of sweats and an old hoodie before padding back into the living room. Ray had his eyes closed while all of the lights in the room were still on. He had fallen asleep attempting to watch the front door from his crunched position on the sofa.

Ember walked over and placed the blanket over his shoulders. She had expected him to jolt awake at the slightest touch, but he appeared too exhausted to notice.

She rolled her eyes and mumbled, "I feel safer already."

Her feet led her to the front door and then over to each window. Ember instinctively checked the locks before she turned off the kitchen lights. She weighed her options and sighed. The small lamp on the side table could stay on, just in case Ray woke up in the middle of the night. Satisfied that Ray wouldn't topple over the low coffee table in the middle of the night, Ember prepared to head back to her room. However, the faintest glimpse of dark ink stopped her in her tracks. Ember spotted the thin licks of ink as they swirled beneath the collar of Ray's shirt.

Odd.

He had appeared so straight-laced that Ember had figured that he would never have something as bold or permanent as a tattoo. She couldn't exactly see the full image, but the small hints managed to spark her curiosity.

Ember decided not to hover and headed over to her bedroom. She closed her door. Her hand momentarily hovered above the metal handle. After a moment of indecision, she pressed down on the lock before heading to bed.

Chapter 17

A pounding from somewhere in the quaint house jolted Ember from her slumber. She sprung from her bed and instinctively grabbed the metal kitchen knife that was hiding behind her small reading chair.

"Ember! Are you okay? You have three seconds before I break down this bedroom door! Now it's two seconds!"

Ray's voice carried a hint of panic. The worry noticeably escalated with every word. Ember's grip near the base of the bat grew slick with sweat. What was on the other side of the door? Was it a trap? Was Ray hurt? Did she even want to find out? Screw it. This was her house.

Ember unlocked her bedroom door and swung it open with such force that it hit the wall with a resounding slam. Not that Ember noticed the impressive sound.

All of her attention was drawn to Ray's paler than usual features. His chest moved rapidly as his muscles visibly tensed. Every cell in Ray's body appeared prepared for action. He swiftly inspected Ember for even the smallest hint of an injury. Satisfied, he charged into her room. Ray opened her tiny closet and then stuck his head underneath her bed.

Ember hollered, "What are you doing?"

His panicked search appeared like a discovery-crazed rampage. No stone left unturned.

At first, Ray didn't answer. Too busy on his quest to secure the premises. He made quick work of the shoebox-sized accommodations and eventually answered, "I needed to see if you were safe."

"Why?"

Ray's weighted pause told Ember everything that she needed to know. Something awful had happened.

Ember swallowed the thick ball in the back of her throat and repeated, "Ray, what happened? Did another woman leave?"

Of all the times to suddenly become frightened of a word, Ember's subconscious had chosen now. The word itself seemed to hold a certain power. An unknown strength that Ember at her core refused to invoke.

"Not exactly a murder, Ember. Come with me."

The severity behind Ray's cryptic words coupled with his guarded gaze made Ember feel lost. What could be so horrible that he struggled to put the problem into words? Apparently, many issues could fit that description if the last few days were a reliable benchmark.

For once, Ember refrained from a snippy remark. She wordlessly followed Ray to the front of the house. Faint rays of morning light entered through the mostly closed bargain curtains. Ray unlocked the door and led Ember out into the yard where lush green grass abruptly turned into unforgiving concrete.

Ember brought a shaking hand to her face and covered her mouth in shock. She refused to believe what she was seeing.

The concrete floor immediately outside of Ember's home was coated in a red substance that was quickly drying an ugly copperish-brown. The substance formed a perfectly scrawled message.

Ember's voice quivered, "Almost perfect."

An assertive voice shouted instructions into the speaker of a phone, but Ember couldn't pry her eyes away from the coppery horror.

One question commanded her full attention. Whose blood was outside of her house?

Chapter 18

Dreams are a funny combination of fact and fiction. They're bits and pieces of reality shaped by the subconscious. Sometimes dreams tell people about a truth that they are too afraid to grasp when awake. Sometimes they describe deeply hidden fears. A place where various realities can float between life and death. Connected to both sides of the coin. A state where anything is possible. Even nightmares.

"This can't be real," Ember muttered the words under her breath as she pressed her nose into the chilled glass of the antique window. The condensation that passed through her lips fogged up the glass, but Ember was too preoccupied to care. This couldn't be real. Nope. It had to be a bad dream. A nightmare.

Ember had always believed that people that experienced intense moments of cognitive dissonance during high-stress situations were unreasonable. It had always made sense to simply accept the situation and move on. It was pointless to stare at the facts while completely frozen in disbelief. However, as Ember watched half of the town's police force scour her yard, she struggled to make the situation feel real. It was as if she was watching her own body from a distance. Ember could see her dark hair, still tussled from sleep and noticed how her hand created the faintest imprint against the window. She had to stand on the tips of her toes to get a useful view of the yard. The main drawback of her lovely casita was that it was designed with a tall person in mind. Hovering just under five feet made it difficult to navigate unreasonably tall windows.

People that Ember didn't recognize from around town hovered near the ominously scrawled words. Complete strangers trailed around the back of her once-sacred house. So far, not a single soul had even bothered to give her an update. That wouldn't do. She pushed back her shoulders and decided to take charge.

Ember had once read a book that described how some people had the power to control their dreams. She had reread that specific chapter with a sense of awe. Ember had never considered that some people had no control over what happened to them in their mind, even when they were asleep. Were they not the engineer of their own dreams? We're they not building imaginary skyscrapers and planning adventures to distant lands with nearly unpronounceable names? Ember had always assumed that everyone could command their dreams. It was reality that had always given Ember trouble.

If this really was a dream, Ember decided to forge ahead. First thing on the agenda? Pants. She stalked into her bedroom and grabbed a pair of jeans from the bottom of her closet. As she turned around, the sensation that something was out of order caused the hairs on the back of her neck to stand on end. Ember paused as the hold that she had on her denim pants grew tighter. Her eyes quickly scanned the room, searching for even the slightest hint of trouble.

"No es posible."

Impossible.

Ember tentatively inched closer to her bed. A small daisy was innocently positioned on her pillow. The seemingly wholesome offering rested on the only pillow that Ember liked to use. She hated frills and found that a single pillow suited her needs just fine. Now, she regretted even having one.

She hovered over the flower placed in the center of the cotton pillowcase. It was impossible to miss. Had Ray decided to enter her room? How had she missed him when she had been right next to the front door? Was she dreaming?

A sharp pinch against the soft flesh of her shoulder confirmed that she was very much awake. She leaned down and noticed that the offending flower had a small note attached to its stem. For a moment, Ember contemplated ignoring it. She needed to get one of the people outside to handle this. Of course, she managed to make it as far as her bedroom door before returning back to her bed.

Ember grabbed a pen from her bedside table and nudged the note open. She tried to make sense of the sparse words that were shakily looped onto the paper, but failed.

"This doesn't make any sense."

Her brows pulled together at the nonsensical words, but Ember knew that it had to be some sort of clue. A piece of the twisted puzzle.

"What's that?" An inquisitive male voice called from the entrance of Ember's room.

Ember noticed how Ray's eyes were locked on the stupid piece of dead plant ruining her bed. She acted before even thinking as she called, "I don't have pants on!"

She swiftly shut the door in his face and hid the letter in a drawer. Ember decided to leave the flower, seeing that it had already been discovered. She shimmied into dark blue jeans that were covered in a hodgepodge of stains and then opened the door.

Ray stood barely two steps away and wasted no time in barging into the room once Ember granted him entry.

"Where's the fire?" Ember defensively crossed her hands over her chest. The snide comment, a reflexive defense mechanism crafted from decades spent needing to break tense silences.

If Ray had heard the words, he made a point not to make note of it. He leaned over the flower as if it was the murder weapon in question. His features turned into a stormy mask as he took out his phone and took a few photos.

"This complicates things."

"Great, I was afraid that things were getting too easy," Ember made a show of rolling her eyes as her heart thrummed to an unsteady rhythm.

Chapter 19

Ember couldn't tell her head from her culo, not that she really cared. The stress was mounting and she fought a deeply ingrained instinct to flee town. Someone was playing with her, but why? Was it really all about one podcast episode? Was it someone from LA that she had stiffed before getting the hell out of dodge? Ember wasn't proud of the debt that she had accumulated before running away, but mierda happens. More accurately, falling into a depression after the death of your only known relative happens.

Tough.

"Ms. Lopez, can you think of any reason why someone might be trying to hurt you?"

Take a number.

The sarcastic words died in the back of her throat. Instead, a well-practiced veneer of confidence and carefully-placed defiance came to the forefront of her expression. Forced nonchalance wasn't going to save her. Her best bet was working with the ragtag team of town do-gooders. The police department was likely running on less than five hours of sleep and a gallon of watered-down breakroom coffee.

Bleak.

Ember glanced around the room and sighed. She was starting to notice new details every time that she entered the police department. Not amazing details containing useful information, but details none-the-less.

The paint on the left hand wall had a slanted pattern while the paint on the wall to Ember's right remained even. Clearly, one painter had been more skilled than the other when covering the room. Heck, maybe the painter had simply grown lazy.

How many people did it take to create a building from start to finish? Ember could guess the obvious culprits like an architect and a contractor, but what about the less obvious jobs? How much time and effort were taken for granted when creating a building? How many people did it take to keep a place running? How many people that performed key tasks in the police department ended up ignored and overlooked?

For example, Madge.

Madge remained the friendly, dependable name that Ember had come to associate with the cheery elderly woman that ran the front desk. The woman in her early 70s handled all of the administrative tasks for the building and its unruly officers. Obviously, Madge was one of the key reasons that the department was still standing. Ember was willing to bet that the tiny woman who was just slightly taller than the desk took charge of most tasks. Madge had to be at least 90% of the reason that the fluorescent lights were still on.

Surely, she managed the majority of work. But who were the other people that helped to keep everything clean and neat? What were the names of the electricians that ensured all of the lights actually stayed on? For such a rundown building, it had to require a sizable group of people to keep it in working order. Right?

Maybe Ember was thinking about this all wrong. Maybe the building was handled exactly how it looked. With aging hands that grew more and more complacent over time. Like an owner that can no longer climb up and down the ladder to fix the gutters. Perhaps age had settled into the department and made it slow. That theory felt more accurate given the spindly cobwebs that crept near the corners of the room. A tiny black dot crept around the room and Ember watched the bug with something close to mild interest. She wondered if the little creature would manage to make a lap before she was finally allowed to leave.

A nasally voice halted Ember's charging train of thought, "Ms. Lopez?"

"Where's Ray?"

"His shift ended several hours ago. He should be back later this week."

Ember folded her arms across her chest and muttered, "Figures."

At least someone was able to take a break. Ember had decided to sleep in her car for the evening. It felt safer to be in a bedroom with wheels. She dreaded the idea of being stranded in a room where the killer had easy access. Her instinct to run also made the idea of a car several times more appealing than a conventional bedroom.

Ember knew that the officers were still scratching their heads, trying to understand how the killer had entered her bedroom undetected. It didn't make any sense. How could someone enter Ember's room while she had stood only a few feet away? Was the suspect that they were looking for a spectral figure? A mutant? La Llorona? The last guess was the most unlikely. Ember didn't have any kids for the legendary angry ghost woman to drown, but still.

"Please focus, Ms. Lopez. This is pretty serious and we are doing our best to protect you," The statement did little to comfort Ember. She observed the man on the opposite side of the table. He appeared maybe two or three years older than 18. He definitely was too young to legally buy a beer. He had the faintest whispers of a patchy attempt at a beard covering his pale skin. A kid. Ember was stuck talking to a kid about potentially getting murdered. Yep, she was definitely going to die.

Ember scrunched her eyes shut as she asked, "Was it human blood?"

The kid visibly bristled at Ember's easy dismissal of his carefully practiced statement. He shifted in his seat and tapped a stack of papers against the side of the desk in a vain attempt to restore order.

The youth tried to discreetly review the various words swiftly typed across the pages. A low humming sound emanated from the back of his throat as he searched. The sound reminded Ember of elevator music.

The youngster seemed about ready to reply. He opened his mouth, but then just as quickly snapped it shut. He provided a bland response, "I'm sorry, Ms. Lopez. Information about ongoing cases is classified."

"The ongoing case is about my house. My podcast. My vida! People are being murdered exactly the way that I described on my podcast. I don't think that it's vain of me to ask about this case. I'd be an idiot not to ask. This killer definitely knows my life. Want to know a secret?"

The kid leaned closer. Curiosity visibly colored his features.

Ember waited until he was only a few inches away before she shouted, "This damn case will most likely involve my death if you don't get it together and help me solve this!"

The last sentence ended at least three octaves higher than the start. Her chest rapidly rose and fell as an intense sliver of irritation swirled around her chest. Ember narrowed her eyes at the cop who was definitely closer to being in a high school economics class than a shooting range.

In response, the kid lowered the stack of papers and defensively narrowed his beady blue eyes. He tapped the table as he pointed out, "I could have you arrested for threatening an officer. You're acting hysterical. I understand that this is a new and frustrating situation, but you are going to need to respect the officers trying to help you. The next outburst will cost you."

This kid could eat shit. The obvious attempt at a paternal tone infuriated Ember. What were they teaching at the police force? Misogyny 101? Incredible.

Ember intentionally lowered her voice so that it carried across the table, just a hair's length longer than a whisper, "Look, I have every right to display emotions when the women of this town are obviously being hunted down by a crazed serial killer. Now, instead of rightfully understanding my justified frustration, you are trying to cow me into being quiet. Which one of us is behaving like a hysterical little boy? The person expressing her clear frustration at an unprecedented situation or the obviously undertrained child that's holding a gun?"

The kid instantly paled at Ember's even words. She had made it a point to deliver each word with as little snark as possible. She simply allowed her furious gaze to speak for itself.

As expected, the kid could not handle even the slightest push against his fragile position. He swiftly stood from his seat as a shaky hand hovered over the top of his holstered gun.

"Don't tell me. You're going to shoot me for telling you that you have no idea how to speak to women? I hate to be the one to tell you, but if you do that then you'll only be proving my point."

Ember remained glued to her seat. Part of her was alarmed that she managed to so easily rattle the newbie's cage. The slight sheen of perspiration on the kid's neck only emphasized his obvious distress. In any other situation, Ember would have laughed or at least told him off for being a jumpy, sexist idiot. Unfortunately, the idiot had a gun and appeared to be deliberating if she was an actual threat.

The rookie's fingers remained just a few inches away from the trigger as he stood and took a few steps away from Ember. He slowly inched around the table as if she was the devil incarnate.

Hell, maybe she was. It wasn't like her behavior exactly earned her a Mother Theresa award.

On the other hand, she was just speaking her mind. Who knew that such candor had the ability to be so damning?

"Josh, you're off the case. You're getting desk work from now on."

A cold voice mercilessly cut the tension within the small room. Ember looked behind her and audibly sighed in relief. Ray was holding two steaming styrofoam cups and staring at the younger officer with barely-restrained fury.

"Out."

Josh left the room with his head down and shoulders slumped. He made it a point to practically touch the wall as he walked around Ray to reach the door. The kid behaved like a naughty dog as he left the room with his metaphorical tail tucked between his legs.

Good. Little jerk.

"What was that all about?"

Ray's voice was tense as he held out a cup of watered down sludge in Ember's general direction. The faintest scent of coffee invaded her frazzled senses.

"I expressed frustration and apparently that's not allowed. Kid got nervous and reached for his gun."

If Ray had any thoughts about the situation, he didn't share them. His face appeared stormy, but he refused to give anything else away. Instead, he took a sip of coffee while his face scrunched up in disgust. Ember wasn't exactly sure if it was the coffee causing his facial muscles to spasm or his frustration. She didn't exactly feel like asking for clarification.

She mirrored Ray's actions and took a sip of the coffee. Ember audibly gagged. She put the cup down and choked out, "This isn't coffee. It's poison."

"You're right. I still haven't found a good place to grab coffee. I'm living off of oatmeal, stale coffee, and regrets."

The admission perked up Ember's ears. She tilted her head to the side and took in the bags under Ray's eyes. The stubble that covered his chin appeared more visible once she took the time to actually look at him. Really see him. He looked like shit.

"I thought your shift ended?"

"It did. I'm here outside of my assigned hours."

Ember teased, "Can't get enough of me?"

"I can't leave you alone for a second without worrying that someone wants to shoot you."

Unoffended, Ember gave a lopsided shrug and then pushed the white cup of potential poison a few inches away from her side of the table.

She tilted her head, "I know an average diner. I used to work at the town's local watering hole. Might need to go back, seeing as I'm unemployed."

"Let's go."

"Perfect. I'd say let me stop at home to get my resume, but it doesn't really matter. It's a small town. Everyone already knows what I've done."

Chapter 20

"It's not poison."

"I told you, already. A little trust would be nice," Ember rolled her eyes and settled deeper into the red booth.

Commotion from the other casual diners settled some of Ember's nerves. Noise meant people and people were witnesses. After so many years living in the city, Ember still struggled to appreciate the stillness of the country. Of course, from what Ray had said, the quiet near her home was particularly unsettling. Even for a small town.

Perhaps some part of her associated intense silence with danger. An unnatural state. A calm before the raging chaos.

The chattering diner with greasy burgers and clanking plates felt like home. Ember took a sip of coffee and sighed in content.

"It's no Coffee King Max, but it will do."

"Can't you just admit that it's substantially better than the liquid tar at the station? I have to admit that I expected more from Madge."

Ray looked away at Ember's cross words. His eyes drifted to the menu as the table fell into silence.

"It wasn't Madge. You tried to make coffee at the station. You brewed us poison!" The accusation in Ember's tone was obvious.

Ray held up his hands as if he was handling a hostile hostage situation. Both palms facing Ember's face as a booming chuckle resounded around the bright red booth.

"Guilty. Read me my rights."

"It's a backwards world. I don't believe I need to read you your rights, anymore. But just for good time's sake. You have the right to always buy me a coffee. Anytime that you decide to make a coffee will be held against you until I decide to drop the grudge or until better coffee is provided."

"Harsh rules. I'll make it right. Who am I to argue against modernized Mirandas?"

"Smart man."

"I'm learning."

The waitress arrived and refilled the two empty cups. Ember turned her head to the right and noticed a pest control truck as it turned into the back of the hamburger joint across the road. The corners of her lips momentarily pulled down into a frown.

"What?"

"They usually arrive before the shop opens to keep customer's tongues from wagging."

"It's nine in the morning, Ember. I'm pretty sure that the Hamburger Happy Hut is still closed."

"Wow, it feels like the day is already over." A wheeze of surprise left Ember's chest. It resembled a defeated sigh, but the silent lament was inaudible. The diner music that seemed stuck in the 1950 managed to drown her out.

"Time is a funny thing. It's more about what happens and less about the when."

"Sometimes it's about the when."

"Sometimes."

"So you're saying quality over quantity?"

"Something like that."

Ember shrugged and turned to look out the window. She watched as the exterminator across the street barely had time to knock before he was swiftly ushered inside of the Hamburger Happy Hut. The owner of the competing greasy spoon poked his head outside the door. He cautiously eyed the street for a potential Nosy Nelly. Apparently, the pest control agent had arrived for more than just a quarterly inspection.

"We're never eating there."

"Whatever you say, Boss."

Satisfied, Ember turned her gaze back to Ray. Their casual conversation offered a welcome break from the chaos, but the inevitable destruction loomed in the air like an impending tornado. It was unavoidable. They both knew that they were in the middle of the storm. Ember decided that it was better to weather the worst of the brunt in public. She needed a space where she could feel safe. Seen. Ideally, even missed.

Her quiet home felt tainted. Violated.

"Do you always treat the people that you're stuck babysitting to the finest diner coffee in the area?"

"No. Just the ones that can't stay out of trouble."

Ember hollered in response to Ray's unexpected quip. He often appeared so serious that any break from the mold was a welcome surprise.

"Did they find anything about the blood?"

"It's human."

Three syllables.

Two simple words.

One closing throat. Ember's hand traveled to her neck as she tried to remember how to breathe. Whose blood was it? Had the killer found another victim? Had the killer used his own blood? Has anyone been reported missing?

"Take a sip of your coffee, Ember." Ray's words were easy enough. Simple instructions to follow.

Ember took a hefty chug of the still somewhat scalding liquid. The burn stung the back of her throat and offered a welcomed distraction from her rapidly darkening thoughts.

"I'm switching to decaf." She grumbled the offhand comment and then nudged, "Anything else?"

"Not yet, but something will come up."

"What makes you say that?"

"It's all so fast."

"You mean it's rushed."

Ray swiveled his head from one direction to the other before he leaned closer to Ember and lowered his voice, "Yes. It's like the killer is leading up to something. This is just the beginning. We're missing the bigger picture."

"You mean we're missing the final move. You're right. The killer is building up to something. So far, all we've been able to do is react. We need to be proactive. Let's start digging into the old records."

"Why?"

"Because history repeats itself. These murders are following an old pattern. Either from the original killer or a copycat that likes my stupid podcast. Either way, we need to know what happened."

The large bell above the diner door chimed in greeting. Ember looked up and noticed the town's newly appointed mayor. The woman donned a smart power suit as she waved to other members in the diner before eventually taking a seat at the counter. The room seemed to drop several decibels as customers attempted to listen to the newly-appointed mayor as she ordered a stack of plain pancakes. Simple and predictable. Ember already liked the woman.

"Ember?"

Ember returned to the moment and ran a hand down her face in pure frustration. No, frustrated wasn't the right word. The emotion that Ember was feeling was likely somewhere in the dictionary, but she struggled to find the word. She often attempted to use English terms that were nearly lost to the past. How could she put into words an experience that she couldn't properly describe? It was a silent robbery. It was an eerie feeling to experience something that felt nonexistent. Perhaps the word had intentionally been erased from current memory. Ember struggled to mourn the loss of something that she didn't know everytime that she was at a loss for words.

Chapter 21

"What are you doing?"

Ray's voice hissed into the darkness and slithered along Ember's senses like an irritated snake.

Ember tumbled into a shallow puddle as she traversed the cobblestone alleyway. It took her several seconds before she eventually reached the back door.

She arched a singular eyebrow and innocently held up a pocket knife and bobby pin, "What does it look like? I'm helping us get inside. We need to look at the files."

A heavy pause settled over the thick brick walls as Ray opened and closed his mouth. He looked like a frustrated fish, struggling for air.

"Move," Ray nudged Ember with his shoulder and then reached into his back pocket. He pulled out a key and glanced over his shoulder as he gave Ember a look that said more than words ever could.

Simply put, his eyes said idiot.

"I forgot that you work here."

"Just get inside. Madge is about to end her shift and the officers usually go up to the front desk to tell her good night. She's more popular than the sheriff."

"So some of them do have souls," Ember muttered as she crept behind Ray's back and entered the police station. At least if they were caught it wouldn't really be breaking and entering. They already had the key.

A catlike smile crept along Ember's lips, "This sure beats jimmying the lock."

Ray whipped his head around for the second time and narrowed his eyes. Ember held her arms up and signaled mock surrender. The two silently navigated the piles of discarded typewriters and chairs using the flashlight feature on Ray's phone. Ember tried her best to move silently around the precariously placed piles of crap. It appeared that the department had an interest in hoarding useless shit.

Ray stopped next to several dusty shelves, stacked with old boxes and files. The side of one shelf mentioned the 1980s. Ember inched over to a different shelf and noticed that a black marker had etched the number 1990 into the corner. Time to dig into the 90s. Entire decades of information had been thoughtlessly tossed together.

Maybe the piles weren't as useless as she had originally thought. She reached out and began to sort through the files.

Dust flitted into the air and tickled the back of Ember's throat. She was sure that the files and paperwork had to have been left alone for at least a decade. Flecks of fine dust moved around within the sparse beam of light and reminded Ember of fine snowflakes just before the start of a lengthy winter storm.

"Find anything?"

"No."

The amount of paperwork wasn't exactly impressive for an entire decade's worth of crime. Of course, the town was notoriously quiet and the lack of documented crimes seemed to only bolster such a sentiment. Ember rifled through another file, but paused once she noticed the silence. Ray had stopped searching.

She glanced over and noticed the deep frown lines drawn along Ray's face. His eyes moved from one side of a particular file to the other.

"What's wrong?"

"This file probably had relevant evidence."

"Had?"

Ray held out the file and showed Ember the ripped out pages. The report had discussed the drowned women, but key details about the collected evidence had disappeared.

Not disappeared. The papers had very obviously been roughly torn out. The pages hadn't gone up in smoke. Someone had intentionally ripped them out.

"Maybe there's more information around here. This room looks like it's about the size of the entire first floor. There has to be something else."

Ray closed the file as his knuckles turned white from the intensity of his grip. He muttered, "What if there is nothing else?"

"There will be. Keep looking," Ember left the rickety shelves and decided to snoop around on her own. Her value brand smartphone didn't exactly offer the same amount of features when compared to Ray's smartphone. Ray's phone looked as if he was trying to see into the future. In contrast, the brightness was permanently set to a dull fluorescent blip on Ember's phone.

Beggars can't be choosers.

Ember shrugged and searched the thick boxes of files stacked on the floor. Her fingers made quick work of the papers and she hoped that the marked dates outside of the boxes were at least somewhat accurate.

A slight shuffle from somewhere deep in the room made Ember tremble, Her fingers began to shake as she tried to increase her pace.

"Please don't be a rat. Please don't be a rat."

Ember refused to look in the direction of the sound. It was one thing to have a strong suspicion, but an entirely different manner to have it confirmed. The sound appeared to be getting closer. The movements were growing more self-assured.

That's one big rat.

Any minute now.

She knew that a massive rat or vermin had to be only a few feet away, but the title of a file locked her body in place. The file had compiled a list of potential suspects related to the murdered women. The papers held all sorts of details pertaining to the three different murders. What were the odds that the cases had to do with a different serial killer? Slim.

"We need to go."

Ember looked up as Ray waved his phone in the direction of the back door. His jaw was tense as the commotion from upstairs continued to increase. The night shift was arriving.

With a quick lunge, Ember scrambled to her feet as her slim fingers clamped the file in a deathgrip. She gave a short wave with the manila file and then paused mid-step.

"What's wrong?"

"You scared off the rat."

"Good," Ray rolled his eyes and tugged Ember out of the dusty corner. It was obvious that the news had only managed to irritate him.

"What? Is the big bad detective scared of rats?" Ember teased in a playful whisper as Ray led them out of the department. He narrowed his eyes and locked the door. It was as if they had never entered in the first place.

"Rats carry disease."

"Lots of animals carry diseases. Have you ever picked up a toddler after daycare?"

Ray sighed as they briskly headed away from the alley, "You don't kill toddlers for carrying diseases."

"Exactly! Because we decided to like toddlers. Toddlers are annoying and smelly, but parents and strangers seem to like them. We like toddlers because they're ours. We hate the rats because they're othered. Did you know that we brought the brown rats here?"

"What?"

"Brown rats aren't native to the Americas. It supposedly first arrived here with the first Europeans on ships. The rats got stuck for the ride. They beat all odds on a floating wooden ship just to be punished for the rest of eternity for existing in a place that they never agreed to go to in the first place. You see what I mean?"

"How do you know so much about rats?" Ray opened the passenger side door and waited for Ember to get settled.

Ember waved a hand near her face, "I was reading up on a lover's revenge murder mystery. Grizzly stuff. Anyways, that's not the point."

Ray turned on the car and playfully arched an eyebrow, "What's the point?"

"The point is that it's not fair to blame an animal for wanting to survive. It's what we were all programmed to do."

The car settled into an uneven silence as Ray weaved around the twisting roads and carefully maneuvered the blind curves. Something told Ember that he was intentionally being more cautious than necessary for her benefit.

"Okay, what is it?"

Ember narrowed her eyes and turned her gaze so that it landed on the side of Ray's face. His jaw was partially cast in shadow as the massive trees reached up to the sky and blocked out the waning winter light.

"Nothing. You're just different than I thought you would be. More introspective."

"I'll take it," Ember settled in the low chair and fussed around with the settings. She needed something to do to avoid putting any weight into Ray's words. The latch on the side of the ancient rental car groaned in protest. No matter how much the man seemed to draw her in, Ember knew the truth. She flicked the latch and the seat lazily tilted back. Ember made no move to raise the seat so that she could once again see over the dashboard.

It was a dark and twisted world and Ember feared that putting any stock into Ray's actions would only disappoint her in the end. It was better to expect nothing. Heck, maybe if Ember said the wrong thing, he'd dropkick her out of the car.

She had decided that they were like two different species. Ember needed to focus on her own survival. No one else would save her.

Like usual, Ember planned to work alone.

Chapter 22

"I don't have any clothes, Ember."

"That's no surprise. You've been wearing the same pair of pants since we met."

A growl intertwined with the words in the back of Ray's throat as he corrected, "That's not true. Can you stop being a smartass for five seconds? I need to go back to my place and grab some clothes."

Ember rose from her hunched position on her sofa. The book that she had been unable to focus on slipped from her fingers and landed on the cushions. She licked her lower lip and shrugged, "I'll lock the doors while you're out."

"That worked so well last time."

"Maybe the second time's the charm," Ember didn't exactly believe what she was saying, but the thought of following Ray back to his place made her palms sweaty. She tossed out the words without actually meaning a single one.

Ray inched closer. He leaned down and Ember could smell the faintest traces of coffee and cologne as they gently weaved around her face. He made sure that Ember's green gaze was locked with his own. He said, "The second time could earn you a body bag."

Chapter 23

"Nothing you are saying will keep you safe, Ember."

Ray's tone halted the protest rumbling up the back of Ember's throat. Ember's argument quickly became stuck like a truck trying to make a u-turn on a gridlocked freeway. It was an inconvenient traffic jam between her mind and her gut. Ember's logic rammed against her intuition like an eight-vehicle pile up.

Ray's voice held no anger. He was simply stating a fact. Describing an undisputed detail. Speaking impartially about Ember's demise which was more than likely going to happen if she continued to behave like a stubborn dumbass. Those weren't exactly Ray's words, but Ember got the point.

Maravilloso.

Ember narrowed her eyes at Ray as she sized him up. She took her time looking at his broad shoulders and sharp chin. Her laser-focused gaze noticed a thin scar that had previously gone undetected. It was camouflaged within his five o'clock shadow.

"You need to shower and grab clothes. I need to stay here and feed the birds."

"Feeding the birds doesn't rank very highly on the scale of priorities."

"They appreciate consistency."

"Sure they do," Ray's words held a generous helping of disbelief.

"Look, you don't get it. Brutus is a temperamental extortionist. If I miss his nightly feeding then he'll riot and take shingles off the roof. I don't have the patience or the funds to deal with that right now."

Ray groaned, "Fine. We stay at your house and feed the damn birds. After feeding the extortionists we will head straight to my place."

"To grab your clothes," Ember felt compelled to clarify Ray's statement. His final sentence had ended on an odd note of finality that had twisted Ember's insides.

"Yes, we're also staying the night. Your house is compromised, Ember."

Compromised was a word people used to talk about their online shopping accounts and mileage-related credit cards getting hacked. Sure, there was also the odd mention of the word in old spy movies, but still. It didn't feel right. The word lacked the exact weight that Ember was currently feeling as it pressed down on her chest. At the end of the day, a stranger had violated Ember's sanctuary. Worse, Ember had been present in the house when it had happened. She had been standing just a few feet away. Completely oblivious. How had someone managed to so deftly navigate around her pint-sized house? Hell, even Ember often tripped over the clumsily positioned potted ficus near her bedroom door.

"Ember?"

"One second. I'm trying to think of another plan."

"There is no other plan," Ray casually folded his arms across his chest, the smug quality in his voice grated against Ember's already thin patience.

"Not yet. I told you to give me a second."

"I don't understand the hold up. It's the next best option. Your home isn't safe, Ember. That's very clear. Besides, I've already seen your place and we still don't know how the killer got in."

"You already had access to my place," Ember didn't need to continue her sentence. The implication behind her words swirled around in the air like an ominous tornado just waiting to touch down on land and create chaos.

Ray's gaze turned guarded as he took a step back. It was as if Ember's sparse handful of words had managed to land an astounding blow against his chest.

Ember wondered if it would have just been simpler to stand in the center of the room while screaming at Ray that he was the killer. She wondered if giving a voice to her concerns that he was the killer would create any less damage than hurling a thinly-veiled implication. The impact appeared to be the same.

However, the whispers in the back of Ember's mind told her not to bother with being polite. She didn't owe Ray any polite behavior or self-sacrificing kindness. So what if assuming that he was the killer insulted him? In the grand scheme of things what was a little insult compared to an actual murder? Wasn't it better to be slightly insulting if it meant being able to live another day?

Ray was the only person with easy access to Ember's home. He knew how her front door creaked with too much weight and had peered into every room under the guise of safety. It was very possible that in all of the confusion, Ember had dismissed his presence. It was possible that Ray had managed to silently slip around the house and enter Ember's bedroom while she had been too busy fogging up the glass of her front window. He had the means to create the perfect distraction and the knowledge to plant the perfect evidence. All he really needed to successfully create an acceptable collection of false clues was Ember's trust. If Ember trusted Ray, then he could guide her attention in any direction that he wanted. The understanding of the situation made Ember's stomach drop to her feet. Was she looking at the killer?

It was possible.

The larger message of the interaction slithered around the room like a venomous snake. It crept between Ember and Ray and whispered soundlessly into the air, *I don't trust you.*

Slowly, Ray nodded his head, "Fair enough. We can feed the birds. Afterwards, you can wait outside of my hotel door while I grab my stuff."

"What do we do once you have your clothes?"

Normally, Ember wasn't one to ask about so many trivial details, but suddenly every single nugget of information felt as precious as gold. Each detail had the potential to be priceless. A single clue could help Ember find the killer or at the very least, collect enough information to survive another day.

"We go to a different hotel. A neutral ground."

Ray noticed how Ember's nose scrunched at his casual statement. He clarified, "I don't exactly live in town. This case was suddenly thrown on my desk. There was no time to make a reservation at the Rice Carlyle." His sardonic tone included just enough sarcasm to quell some of Ember's misgivings. It made sense that Ray would be staying at a hotel. Now they just needed to find another place that offered temporary accommodations in a town with a population less than 10,000.

Facil.

"There is another place in town. It's called The Snuggly Inn."

Ray's brows pinched together so Ember hastily added, "It's old, but it's clean. The bed sheets and linens won't kill you, but Donna's cooking just might."

"Who's Donna?"

"She's the tiny widow that runs the place. We got to know each other when I first came to town. Her nightly rates are fair."

Now it was Ray's turn to become suspicious, he tilted his head to the side and parroted, "You came here without having a place to stay?"

Leading question. Ember circumvented the task and quipped, "That makes two of us."

"Ember, you're going to need to at least tell me some information about your life. To some extent, you're going to need to trust me and confide at least partially in me. It's obvious that the murderer knows you. You only have one shot at beating this lunatic. Whether you like it or not, everything that you do and everything that you've ever done has the ability to come into play. Now just tell me, how do you want the final score to look?"

Ray's features were serious and he uncrossed his arms as he gestured up in the sky at an invisible scoreboard. At that moment, it appeared that they were both playing a losing game. The killer was winning.

"I think sport analogies are bullshit, but I'll play ball."

Chapter 24

"How many shirts do you need?"

"If you keep bugging me then I'll just pack extra slowly. You can freeze outside while I take my time picking outfits from the warmth of this two-star hotel room."

"That's really mature! This is technically a motel," Ember leaned around the doorframe and hollered into the room. Her feet remained firmly planted outside of the carpeted room as she stuck her head inside to yell at Ray.

Ray looked up from the wooden drawers near the corner of the room. He wagged his finger in a similar fashion to a parent scolding an impatient child, "Did I bother you when we went to your house and fed the birds?"

At first, Ember didn't reply.

"Ember?"

Like a petulant kid, Ember kicked the side of the door and then scuffed the heel of her shoe against the concrete floor. Her toes refused to touch the carpeted floor on the other side of the door. She hated that Ray was being reasonable.

Feeding the crows had not been a simple or quick task. Especially since the birds had decided to leave gifts. Today's trinkets of appreciation included two shotgun shells. Explaining that the shells did not actually belong to a gun that Ember owned had been tricky to say the least. It was an excuse several steps more far-fetched than a dog eating homework. Ember was already under suspicion for murder and now her yard was sporadically littered with bullet casings. Talk about a public image crisis.

"Fine. Take your time planning the perfect matching outfit," Ember muttered.

The drive from the rundown motel to the well-loved inn took less than ten minutes. Mostly because the roads were isolated and Ray tended to have a lead foot when taking curves. The trees by the car spun together in a kaleidoscope of branches. The light from the car's head beams reflected off the white stripes of paint on the side of the road.

All too soon, the Snuggly Inn's large wooden bear came into sight. The carved creature stood tall as one paw remained permanently raised in greeting.

"Cute bear."

"That's Snuggles."

"The wooden bear has a name?"

"It's a loving nickname that was given to the statue by the town kids several decades ago. Guess it stuck."

Ray turned the car into a parking lot and selected one of the available spots near the main office. A white neon sign sat in the corner of the window and indicated vacancy. The light flickered in time to Ember's heartbeat.

The smell of harsh cleaning products and cinnamon sticks instantly assaulted Ember's nose as she opened the front door. A bell tinkled above the door. Ray had to awkwardly shuffle inside the small room.

    A thin cloud of white hair appeared just a few inches above the wooden counter. It seemingly floated closer as faint footsteps padded against the carpeted floor. The petite figure climbed the small stepping stool and revealed a kind, weathered face.

    "It's so good to see you again, Ember! You even brought a friend," the older woman chirped as she rocked back and forth on the stepping stool that allowed her to see over the countertop.

    Against Ember's better judgment, she allowed the faintest hint of a smile to creep along the corners of her lips. Donna's motherly behavior always managed to put Ember at ease. It also helped that Donna had the least threatening demeanor of anyone in town.

    Donna added, "What can I do for you, Sweet Girl?"

    Ember reached out and instinctively gripped Donna's wrinkled hands. She never considered herself a touchy person, but something about Donna's sweet disposition made Ember want to connect on a more meaningful level.

    Bleh.

    Ignoring her own disgust, Ember swallowed down the lump in her throat. She admitted, "I've been better Donna, but you know how it is. How's the inn? Is it turning around?"

Creases formed near the corner of Donna's eyes as a proud grin illuminated her face, "I finally saved up enough money to look into the ant problem. Hopefully the little buggers never come back!"

"That's perfect! I was wondering if the tiny energy drink thieves were still around."

"Tiny energy drink thieves," Ray muttered in the background. Ember ignored his off-handed comment and kept her attention focused on her old friend.

"I'm more than happy to hear that they're gone and out of sight."

"In the process of being gone. Pest control is making a few rounds."

"Close enough. That's still better than when we started."

Donna nodded pleasantly, "What can I help you with, Sweetheart?"

"Can we have two rooms?"

Donna's lower lip thinned as her face grew pinched with displeasure. She sighed, "I don't have two adjoining rooms."

"What about rooms that are across the hall from each other?"

"No, sorry. You're really striking out today, Hun."

Ember was about to make a witty remark, but she decided against it. She noticed how Donna's brows pulled together at an odd angle. Perhaps her brows were a centimeter or two too far away to properly convey a sincere apology. Of course, it was possible that every other room was being fumigated. It was also possible that Ember was reading too much into a simple inconvenience.

A deep voice suddenly pulled into the center of the conversation. Ray began, "We'd really like to have two rooms that are either across the hall or share a wall."

"I have rooms available on opposite ends of the hallways. Two rooms to a hallway so that the center rooms can be thoroughly cleaned. I suppose that the distance will make sharing toothpaste nearly impossible."

The lighthearted joke did little to settle Ember's growing suspicions. Damn it, Donna. Of all the times to start meddling, this was definitely a top ten worst. Not that the older woman seemed bothered in the least. In fact, the faint smile behind Donna's gaze told Ember everything that she needed to know.

Well played, Donna. Ember thought as she defensively folded her arms over chest and prodded, "Well what options do we have, Donna? You really have us at your mercy."

The play on words hid their obvious disagreement. Ray appeared perfectly unaware of their thinly-veiled argument.

"What about a room with two queen beds?"

Ember's voice climbed an octave in displeasure as she pressed, "The other option?"

"I have one room with two queen beds. Otherwise, I have several rooms left with king sized beds. The king beds are just as comfortable and the rooms have a generous amount of closet space if that's a concern."

Before Ray could bungle them into falling for Donna's cellophane-thin matchmaking plan, Ember declared, "Okay, the room with the two queen beds is perfect. Please."

Donna swiftly nodded her head. Ember nudged Ray's shoulder when Donna mentioned the room deposit.

"Oh, so now I'm needed."

"Yup. I'm unemployed until my name is cleared. This investigation has made my life extremely inconvenient. If I get a job then I'll pay you back for half."

Ray's gaze narrowed, "You did not need any help from me getting into this mess. It was all you, but I really appreciate your interest in trying to include me."

Ember looked away, "You're welcome."

Her gaze settled on the tired dull red oblong-patterned carpet. It had likely been placed in the entrance during the late 80s. A relic stuck in time. Ember understood only too well how it felt to be stuck. She was a cornered stray, ready to turn tail and run away at the slightest gesture of kindness. What could a handful of generous scraps really mean? What were the rules? Rather than skeptically accepting the kindness, Ember often retreated back to the safety of her own demons. Afterall, the devil that you know.

    The hallways looked just like the last time that Ember had stayed at the inn. She couldn't put her finger on it, but there was only a slight difference. A sickly sweet scent hung in the air and filled Ember's chest. Ember discreetly mumbled a few obscenities into the collar of her shirt. She deeply inhaled the scent of her dollar-brand laundry detergent. It was a familiar olfactory anchor in an unfamiliar land. The comfortable starkly contrasted the unknown.

    Ray tapped his pocket where he had slid the two old-fashioned keys. He questioned, "Did you hear that?"

    "What?"

    "Exactly. This hallway is dead silent. I bet that we are the only guests on the entire floor."

    Ember gazed from one side of the hall to the other. She did a quick tally of the doors, "There's only five rooms in this hall. Donna also only likes to keep one wing in rotation at a time. This place has a total of three floors with two wings. I'm willing to bet that Donna really only had a few rooms available."

    Ray handed Ember the room key and asked, "Why are you saying it like that?"

    "No reason."

"You're telling me that you don't trust the sweet old lady that owns this place?" Ray turned around and tapped the top of his roomkey against Ember's shoulder.

"I did not say that, but since you brought it up, yes. I just have my suspicions."

Ray sighed as he pushed open the door. Darkness seemed to leak out of the room. It was as if the nothingness was just waiting for an opportunity to consume the light in the hallway. Ember had the odd feeling that they would be gonners if the power suddenly flicked off. One shortage in the power would allow the darkness to spread, unchallenged by the light.

Ember faintly recalled the tall tales that her abuela had told her. Her grandma had loved sharing stories while nestled around an old wooden coffee table. Her grandmother had switched between fluent Spanish and accented English to tell her tall tales. The translated versions were rough and often lacked the rich details of the original tale. The language barrier created an impressively sized wall. Its sheer size was impossible to navigate when attempting to convey the true meaning of a story.

How could you explain an old terror in a language that had never struggled to name it for the very first time? How could you convey a monster in a language that had never once observed its true form? The shifting of tongues was only rivaled in difficulty by the changing mindset associated with the differing cultures. The distinct cultural mindsets molded and colored the collective experience of the language. Without knowing, each generation birthed new words and simultaneously slayed the obsolete.

    Ray reached out a hand and bravely inspected the darkness. His shoulders bunched as he reached into the room. Suddenly, the darkened hotel room became filled with light.

Chapter 25

"I'm going to have a long talk with Donna."

"She's old, Ember. It's very likely that she got the numbers on the keys confused. Don't go back and embarrass her. I'll sleep on the chair."

"Some people only forget when it's convenient for them."

Ray waved a hand in the air as he walked deeper into the room and called, "Here we go."

Ember didn't like what Ray's tone was implying. He found her to be a skeptic of every person's character. A pessimist. Probably a bitch. The odds were high that Ray found her to be all three. The probability of such an assumption being true was also unreasonably high. Usually, Ember didn't care if people found her difficult or distrustful. Especially when at one point or another her distrust had been proven correct.

She wasn't in the mood to contemplate why Ray's words had managed to hurt worse than an unexpected bee sting. Three simple words made Ember want to let the subject go, but deep down she knew that she was right. Donna had switched the rooms on purpose. Of course, Donna hadn't intended anything malicious. She was simply an old woman hellbent on executing a matchmaking mission to find the most difficult person in town a suitable companion.

    Ember looked up from the worn carpet and noticed that the room had a king sized bed placed in the center of the room. Bright red crept along the base of Ember's neck and swirled up to her ears. Luckily, her tan complexion managed to camouflage the most obvious signs of her discomfort. Ray walked around the bed as if it was littered with bed bugs. He gave it a wide berth while he stomped around to inspect the closet.

    "It's pretty large. Reminds me of my dorm room back in college."

    "Let me see," Ember closed and latched the room door before she ambled over to the closet. It appeared that Donna was true to her word. The closet could easily fit a small twin sized bed with enough room for a tiny dresser. What had the designers been thinking?

    "What a waste of space. That could have made a nice living area."

    "A detective with an eye for interior design. Now I've seen it all."

    "Look, I'm on the road most of the time. When I do get the time to sit down and watch tv with a beer then I make sure not to watch a crime show. House Hoopla Network is available in most hotel rooms and it's fun to bet on how many couples will actually survive working together on a housing project."

Ember nudged Ray out of the way as she did a quick spin around the closet. She found herself suddenly more aware of Ray's even breathing. Dark circles clung under Ray's observant eyes and the fluorescent light seemed to dig the grooves deeper into his pale skin. He casually leaned against the doorframe and the poorly hidden power behind his frame offset the visual image of his temporary exhaustion.

"You can take the bed tonight."

"What?"

"You get the bed, Ray. It's your lucky day. You get the bed in a rundown inn all to yourself."

Ray tilted his head in Ember's direction, but didn't follow her further into the compact space. He shook his head, clearly confused by Ember's sudden shift in the conversation.

"Why? Is there something wrong with the bed?"

"You have so little faith in me, Ray."

"Apparently, the feeling is mutual."

Ember dismissively waved her hand in the air as she sidestepped around Ray's form. The closet suddenly felt too crowded. She shook her hand in the air and hunkered down into the wooden desk chair. It creaked in protest and Ember quickly stood. She didn't want to get into trouble for breaking one of Donna's chairs. The last thing that Ember wanted to do was create further damage. It seemed like everywhere she went, people were stuck picking up the mess. How many women were going to die? Did the killer already have his next victim?

Tears of frustration pricked at the back of Ember's eyes. The salt burned her skin. She rubbed her palms against her face in an attempt to physically fight off the wet rivulets that threatened to fall onto the carpet.

"I'm going to find a vending machine. Do you want anything?"

"Water."

"Will do. If I'm not back in ten then send a detective to look for me."

"That's dark."

"You should see my humor," Ember kept her back turned to Ray as she headed out the door. She didn't want to show him the obvious mist that was clouding her eyes. Ember just needed a minute. The weight in her chest felt unreasonably heavy as she ambled down the hall.

"Just breathe. Breathe and pull it together. Panic won't help you. Get some junk food in your belly and start planning," The mini peptalk was the best that Ember could muster on such short notice as she took the stairs two at a time.

She ended up outside. Ember had accidentally walked out of the building and ended up in the corner of the parking lot. The stairs had led her to the back of the inn. Movement near the entrance of the main office caught Ember's attention. She took a step back and hid within the shadows that clung to the sides of the building.

A man with a handful of tools and containers headed into the main office. Ember noticed a large van, parked on the opposite side of the lot. The passenger side door had a sticker shaped in the form of a rat. A fat red criss cross pattern was placed over the top of the rat. It had to be the exterminator that Donna had mentioned earlier.

Curious, Ember snuck a glance at her phone and noticed that it was almost midnight. What was an exterminator doing working at such odd hours? Worse, what was poor Donna doing up so late?

Ember clung to the shadows as she crept closer to the main office. She was sure that several vending machines were located around the area. The small market inside of the inn had already closed several hours ago. Guess value-pack candy and questionable beef jerky would have to do.

The empty main office momentarily made Ember pause. She narrowed her eyes and inspected the room. Stacks of papers were neatly tucked into tall piles behind the counter. Upbeat elevator music played in the background as every trace of the exterminator appeared to have vanished. A shiny object located on the empty counter managed to catch the light. The metallic screwdriver appeared much sturdier than the ones that Ember had purchased for simple house chores.

"Weird," Ember's stomach rumbled and motivated her to continue on her journey. After a few minutes of searching, a row of three vending machines came into sight. The ice machine stood on the opposite wall and rumbled with a vengeance. It likely hadn't been used in ages, but it still had cold air coming from the lid. Ember pulled out a few crumpled dollars from her back pocket and peered into the glass cases. The selection was sparse, but still somewhat manageable.

She decided to get a few sweet and salty options to hedge her bets. Chips, meat sticks, and a chocolate bar. She looked down at her little makeshift collection and groaned, "Agua."

Ember pressed the digits for water and a bottle clattered to the bottom of the machine before stopping short. Damn it. She tried to shake the water loose, but that didn't work. In fact, it seemed that the action had only made the water bottle's position worse.

Deflated, Ember headed in the direction of the main office. Maybe Donna was back at the front desk and could help dislodge the water. Usually, Ember would have just bought another item with the hope of dislodging the first. Unfortunately, she had spent all of the dollars in her wallet. She didn't have enough change to wrangle a heavier item.

Ember poked her head into the main office and sighed. The music had morphed into a more upbeat pop song from the early 2000s. The screwdriver left alone on the counter practically screamed Ember's name. She walked over and tentatively weighed her options.

    Curious, Ember pulled down her sleeves and grabbed the metallic handle with the cotton material of her shirt. She figured that Donna had likely forgotten the object when running around the inn. Ember decided to make a mental note to return it to the old lady in the morning. Hopefully, the tool was long enough to reach into the machine and dislodge the trapped bottle of water.

    Ember left the office just as the curtain shielding the back room from the rest of the office rustled.

Chapter 26

Ember trotted back to the room with the screwdriver in her back pocket and a cold bottle of water tucked under her arm. She felt like a naughty kid, unsupervised in a local candy tienda. Ember was the perfect mix between excitement and mirth as she strode down the hallway, taking two steps at a time.

The candy and junk food threatened to fall onto the once heavily trafficked floor. She awkwardly shuffled from one foot to the next in an effort to free her room key from the confines of her tiny front pocket.

"Why the shit are front pockets so tiny? What jackass designed women's pants to be so useless?"

The door swung open and Ember hastily took a step back. Ray had changed into a pair of low rise sweats and a pullover sweater while Ember had been out searching for food. He grabbed a few packets of sweets that were threatening to fall from Ember's grip and teased, "No wonder you needed to start a podcast. You're always talking to yourself. It's just a constant stream of mental notes."

"My abuela used to say that it was endearing."

"I never said that it wasn't."

The mood within the room subtly shifted. It was so imperceptible that Ember barely noticed it in her mind, but somewhere in her chest the slightest flutter occurred.

They laid out the treasure trove of snacks on the old desk. Her selection of snacks was more disjointed than she had thought.

"Two packs of chips, two sticks of beef jerky, and one chocolate bar," Ray organized the makeshift dinner. The snacks were perfectly aligned like culprits in a criminal lineup. The image of Ray bossing around people all day while on the job pulled at the corner of Ember's mouth. When they first met, he really had a stick up his butt. To be fair, Ember had been brought in for questioning about a murder. It seemed only fair that Ray had been guarded. Ember fleetingly wondered if that was his default setting when at work.

"It's like a Vegas buffet," Ray snickered as he opened the bottle of water. He glanced at Ember's chapped lips and handed her the bottle, "Drink."

"Thanks."

Ember couldn't remember the last time that she had drank water. Maybe yesterday afternoon? It didn't matter.

She returned the bottle and then plucked a bag of extra salty chips from the pile. The plastic compressed until the air exploded out of the bag with a loud pop. Ember flinched at the sound as it echoed around the faded walls.

If Ray noticed her skittish behavior, he was kind enough to feign obliviousness. Ember stuffed a few grease-covered wafers into her mouth. She rubbed her eyes as her shoulders slumped with exhaustion.

"Here, take the bed."

Ray chomped into a stick of jerky and double-checked the lock on the door. To be safe, he lifted the desk chair with one arm and then propped it underneath the door handle. He tested it a few times to make sure that the elongated door handle would get stuck on the chair if anyone tried to open the door.

"Okay, you've baby-proofed the room. Let's go to bed."

Ray chuckled at Ember's beautification of the situation. His fingers dipped to the hem of his pullover sweater. He carelessly tossed it onto the desk and then grabbed the spare linens from the closet that could comfortably cover Ember's bed at home about two times over.

"Where are you going?"

The question was rhetorical. Ember knew exactly where Ray was going. It wasn't like there were many options.

"You're heading to bed so I'm giving you space."

"So you plan to sleep in the tub?"

Ray winced, it was definitely not the best option. The approximate time frame since the last time that the tub had been thoroughly cleaned seemed murky, at best. Yuck.

"Maybe the closet. It's big enough," Ray attempted to force some levity into his tone, but it fell flat.

He was too damn bulky to sleep on the carpet. Ember sighed, "You sleep on the left side of the bed. If you come too close when I'm sleeping then I'll kick you in the balls."

Ember kept her gaze focused on the white sheets. She was still wearing the same outfit from earlier in the day. The grime and dirt seemed to seep into her pores from the well-worn items. Damn.

"Fair enough," Ray ambled to the opposite side of the bed and lifted up the covers. He arched a brow, You're not getting in."

"I hate wearing jeans to bed."

"You forgot to bring sleeping clothes?"

Ember crossed her arms, "No. I decided to sleep in jeans because it's so much easier to relax when wearing restrictive clothing."

Ray held up his hands and made a gesture that signaled something close to surrender. He mumbled, "So grumpy. Just wear my clothes. I packed extra."

The faintest hint of a smile pressed at the edges of Ember's lips as she teased, "I knew you were packing for two."

"Only by accident."

Ember walked into the closet and unzipped Ray's duffel bag. A smirk danced along Ember's features as she looked at the carefully folded clothes. The rows appeared to have military precision. She ran her index finger along the rows of fabric and eventually landed on what appeared to be a long blue shirt and dark sweats.

A faint glimmer near the bottom of Ray's bag caught Ember's attention. She angled the bag into the light and realized that it was the handle of a gun. The gun was neatly placed on top of several meticulously folded pairs of socks. For a moment, Ember had the intense compulsion to reach in and grab it. She could sleep with it under her pillow and use it just in case Ray ended up getting handsy. Worse, what if the murderer appeared in the middle of the night?

Ember held her breath. She had a choice to make and fast. With that said, had she recently been making any good choices? Currently, most of her ideas seemed to end in death.

"Estoy loca."

Ember changed her clothes at lightning speed and then headed back to the bedroom. A booming laugh reverberated around the room.

"What's so funny?"

"It looks like you stole those clothes from a mannequin during a blackout."

"That's descriptive."

"My pants are on the carpet," Ray deadpanned as an impish grin spread across his face.

Ember blanched as she looked down and realized that he was right. Ray's stupid enormous pants had managed to fall to the floor.

"They didn't have a drawstring," Ember could feel heat creeping up the back of her neck as she desperately tried to keep her composure. Her sentence sounded more angry than embarrassed which Ember secretly preferred.

"It's fine. Look, my shirt is long enough that it's touching your knees. Think of it as a really ugly sundress."

Ember stepped out of the pants and placed them on the desk. She mumbled, "I don't wear sundresses."

"Well, tonight you do."

Unwilling to argue, Ember walked around to her side of the bed. She slipped into the covers and then vigorously fluffed her pillow. Once satisfied, she glanced over at Ray and pointed a finger in his general direction, "Your side."

"Will do."

Ember turned off the lamp. The room was basked in the distant glow of fluorescent bathroom light. It peaked out of the partially closed door and cast faint shadows along the room. The miniscule light managed to keep the darkness at bay and helped settle Ember's mind. She reasoned that at least with the light on, she'd be able to decipher the outline of an intruder.

Her grip on the thin sheets tightened as she listened to Ray's heavy breathing. From his sporadic movements, Ember could tell that he was still trying to get comfortable.

"Ray."

"Yeah?"

"You better not snore."

"No promises."

Chapter 27

"You promised!"

Ember's voice took on an octave that was so high-pitched that she was sure that only dogs could hear. She pressed against Ray's warm chest and was instantly greeted with cold as the room's frigid air nipped against her exposed skin.

Ray's voice was thick with sleep, "I did. I kept my promise."

The way that he had emphasized certain words nearly escaped Ember's attention in her slumber-induced haze. She blinked her still bleary eyes and looked over at the other side of the bed.

Nope. Ember decided that she definitely needed to change her name and leave town. Apparently, she had moved to Ray's side of the bed while asleep. Tentatively, Ember reached out a hand and felt her side of the bed. Mierda. It was cold.

"You didn't kick me to the other side?"

Confusion laced into Ember's words as she sat in an upright position with the sheets jostled around her tanned thighs. Her hair probably looked like one of the nests that the crows liked to make in the tall oak trees near her house.

"No. Pull up the sheets. You're letting the cold in."

Ember tugged up the sheets, but refrained from resting against the pillows. Her back remained rigid as she stared at nothing in particular. The silence was calm and Ember didn't bother moving to the cold side of the bed. She sat only a few inches away from Ray. His warmth was a welcomed addition to the freezing room. She'd never admit it out loud.

After a while, Ray sighed and stood from the bed. He stretched and then cleaned up for the day. He returned fully dressed and held Ember's car keys in his right hand.

"Where are you going?"

"To get us a real breakfast. I can't stomach more expired jerky. Do you like donuts?"

A playful grin curled along the corners of Ember's lips. She tilted her head to the side and looked at Ray as he removed the chair from underneath the door knob.

"What?"

"A cop asking for donuts. Isn't that a little too on the nose?"

Ray barked, "Fine. I'm getting bagels. Lock the door."

The door slammed with a sharp bang and Ember was left alone with her thoughts. She quickly skittered across the room to lock the door and then jumped back into bed. She inhaled the fresh scent of pine. Ember curled up on the warmest section of the bed and decided to rest her eyes.

Chapter 28

A firm knock roused Ember from bed. She looked around the room and noticed that she couldn't exactly tell the time of day. The room was placed within the interior of the building so it had no windows. A fact that Ember processed on the way to the door.

She was about to unlock the top latch, but her fingers faltered. Her hand froze only a few inches away from the lock. What if it wasn't Ray? Ember sped over to the closet and looked around Ray's travel bag for his gun. Her brows pulled together once she realized that it was missing.

"Of course he would take it with him," Ember quickly searched around the room for a weapon. What could she use?

A louder knock on the door sent a prickling sensation down the back of Ember's spine as she rushed into the bathroom. She reached up and pulled down the metallic shower rod. The shower curtain crumbled to the floor as Ember gripped the long metal rod between her sweaty palms.

"It's just an extra long baseball bat. I can use this."

Another pound came from the door, but this time it was different. A worried voice called, "Ember? Are you okay?"

Relief filled Ember's chest. She checked the smudged peephole just to be sure before she unlocked the door.

Donna stood only a few inches away. Her thin white hair was safely tucked behind a sleep hat. The older woman donned thick glasses that managed to take up half of her face. In any other situation, Ember probably would have poked some fun at her elderly friend.

However, the intense look of trepidation that was plastered across Donna's features made Ember worried. Donna shifted her weight from one foot to the other as she anxiously rubbed the back of her arm.

"Ember, there's been an accident."

"Accident?"

"Yes, your companion. He just called the inn from the hospital."

"The hospital?"

"Yes, he was in a car accident, but said that he's fine aside from a few bruises. He mentioned something about bagels, but I didn't catch it. I'm afraid that I was still waking up when he started barking instructions down the phone line," Donna shrugged her shoulders in apology as she wrapped the floral patterned robe closer to her body.

"It's perfectly fine, Donna. Thank you for letting me know. What time is it?"

Donna fumbled around in the pockets of her robe before she retrieved an old fashioned flip phone. She held the phone a few inches away from her face as she read, "A few minutes after eight in the morning."

"Wow, it's still early."

"I'll get dressed and check out before going to the hospital," Ember didn't want Donna to think that she was taking advantage of her by holding the room for longer than necessary. Unfortunately, Ember wasn't exactly sure how long she would be stuck at the hospital.

Donna's eyes widened in disbelief as she furiously wagged a finger back and forth. The older woman's lips pulled into a scowl, "You will do no such thing. Keep the room for as long as you need. It's not like I'm in danger of running out of rooms."

Relief flooded Ember's body as she gave Donna a small appreciative smile, "Thank you."

"Don't mention it."

Donna nodded her head before her eyes traveled to the thin metallic bar that Ember was still clutching for dear life. Donna pushed her glasses onto the bridge of her nose, "What are you holding, Ember?"

Chapter 29

"You brought bagels," Ray's tone held a hint of shock as Ember walked closer to his hospital bed.

"You said that it was just a scratch," Ember narrowed her eyes as she noticed the sling on Ray's arm as he sat propped against a sea of white pillows.

"Give or take a broken bone. What's in the bag? I'm starving," Ray gestured with his one good hand to the large paper bag and the two precariously balanced cups of coffee. The cups were about two sizes too large for the small holder and Ember was trying her best not to spill.

"Tell me what happened first and then I'll feed you."

Ray rolled his eyes, "You're withholding food. I'm pretty sure that's a war crime."

Ember gave a careless shrug as she placed the cup holder on the side table and dragged a chair closer to Ray's bed. She quipped, "Write me up. I already have a reputation with the law. A rap sheet a mile long."

"You don't have a rap sheet. You're just a person of interest."

"Same shit," Ember put the large bag on her lap and then shook it in Ray's general direction.

"I ran off the road."

"Your car insurance is going to love you."

Ray's gaze hardened as he angled his body in Ember's general direction and growled, "This isn't funny, Ember."

"I know."

"Listen, I was driving your car."

She sighed and crossed one ankle over the other, "I have insurance."

"No, Ember. I was driving your car. I'm pretty sure that someone was trying to get to you. It wasn't me that they were after."

"They?"

"I didn't see who did it, but you know what I mean."

"Do I?"

Ember opened the bag and tilted it so that Ray could see all of the bagels from his position in the hospital bed.

Ray laughed, "Did you buy out the entire store?"

"I panic ordered."

"What?"

"I panicked when I was ordering the bagels and bought about six. You can have five."

Ray's eyes looked as big as saucers as he sputtered out, "I have never heard of panic ordering, but I'm glad that it happened."

"Donna didn't understand what you had said about the bagels. I went to the shop and bought six before walking over."

"You walked?"

"The town is small, Ray."

A frown managed to mar Ray's features as he scolded, "I was just run off the road by a person likely trying to harm you and your bright idea was to walk alone to a bagel shop before most stores in this sleepy town are even open?"

Ember rolled her eyes as she cut open an egg bagel, "When you put it like that then yes it does sound stupid."

She didn't look away from her task as she globbed on a generous helping of cream cheese to her bagel. Ray had already managed to finish half of an everything bagel. He reached into the bag for a second without bothering with any cream cheese.

Commotion came from the hall. Within seconds, a stern looking white-haired nurse entered the room. She proudly held a clipboard in one hand while she strode into the room with an air of practiced confidence. Ember could already tell that it wasn't this nurse's first rodeo.

"Hi, I'm Nurse Kit. Sometimes the name is Old Witch, but it really depends on who you talk to around here."

The joke eased the tension in the room as Nurse Kit walked over to Ray's bed and checked his vitals. A grin crept along the edges of Ember's lips. She instantly appreciated the older woman's dark sense of humor. It managed to brighten the mood. Ember licked a bit of cream cheese as it threatened to fall off the side of her bagel.

Ray greeted, "Nice to meet you. Would you like a bagel?"

The odd question momentarily caught Nurse Kit off-guard. Her pen paused halfway to the sheet of paper. She glanced up and grinned, "I just had breakfast, but thank you. In my thirty years as a nurse, that's my first time being offered a bagel."

"There's a first time for everything," Ember decided to join the conversation as she handed Ray a warm cup of black coffee.

Ray took a sip and grimaced, "Thanks."

Nurse Kit looked over at Ray and asked, "Are you in pain?"

Ray coughed before he honestly replied, "No. The coffee is just a little strong."

Ember rolled her eyes, "You're a big baby."

"No bullying the patient."

"Scout's honor," Ember gave a vague gesture to her chest and then took a big chug from her own cup of coffee. She smacked her lips together and then looked at Ray.

"Okay, Kids. I looked over your vitals and you should be fine. The arm is fractured, but I am willing to bet that it will heal within the next five weeks. The doctor will be in to see you in a bit."

"Thanks, do you know when I'll be released?"

"I can't officially say, but unofficially, I wouldn't be surprised if you left later today."

"Good."

Nurse Kit walked over to the door and called, "But you didn't hear it from me."

"We didn't hear a thing," Ember called between chewing the last bite of her bagel.

The door shut and Ember tilted the napkin so that she could pour the last few crumbs into her mouth. Ray looked over and sighed, "Take another bagel, Ember. That just looks sad."

Ember grabbed another bagel and pouted, "It's chocolate chip."

"So? Just put it back in the bag and get another one."

"I don't want to put something back that I've already touched."

Ray took in a deep inhale as if the conversation was trying his patience. It probably was.

"Look, just take a different one. I don't care and we are the only two people sharing this bag."

Ember narrowed her eyes at Ray as if searching for the slightest hint of deceit. Once satisfied, she swapped out bagels. She bit into the new one and groaned in content.

Ray leaned back into the mountain of pillows and closed his eyes. He asked, "Which one was that?"

"Garlic."

"Makes sense."

"I don't know how to take that comment so I'm going to ignore it."

Ember looked over and watched as the corners of Ray's mouth quirked into a lopsided smile. She rolled her eyes and took another bite while rising from the wooden chair.

She looked out the window and a chill ran down her spine. Ray's room directly faced the cemetery. Ember discreetly pulled one section of the curtains closed to block the dreary view from Ray's line of sight.

"What are you doing?"

Ember continued to face the window as she explained, "If someone really did push you off the road then there's no reason to keep the window open. We aren't putting on a free show in this room."

"Fair enough," Ray mumbled as his eyes drifted shut.

Ember quietly snuck out of the room. She decided to go hunting for clues while Ray was temporarily out of commission. It was the perfect opportunity to collect some information without a pesky babysitter breathing down her neck. She knew that she'd need to be quick. Ray was going to be pissed if he realized what she was doing. Oh, well.

Better to beg for forgiveness, right?

Chapter 30

Ember aimlessly wandered down the long sterile hallway. Doctors and nurses bustled from one area of the hospital to the next. Each with a clear purpose. The town was relatively small so most of the patients seemed to have sprained ankles or a pesky cough. A few kids seemed to be waiting for their parents. For a moment, Ember wondered what it would feel like to have such a clear sense of purpose. Everything felt so uncertain. Most days it felt like Ember was simply trying to make it to the next. Floating.

"Does your friend need anything?"

Ember turned to her left and noticed Nurse Kit positioned in the center of the hallway. The friendly older woman appeared like a battle-hardened pro as she surveyed the movement within the wing with a steady glance. She quickly took in the organized chaos from one end of the hall to the other. Nothing escaped her attention within the confines of the bright white walls.

"He's good. I just wanted to get out and stretch my legs. The last few days have been a little tough."

"I am sure that they have, Ember."

Ember's face instantly paled. She instinctively took a step back, "How do you know my name?"

Nurse Kit placed a bony hand on her hip, "It's a small town. We have a murderer running free and your podcast is currently raising all sorts of hell from the gossip mill."

Ember scratched the base of her neck. It suddenly felt like the other patients were too close and the doctors were too near. Why was Nurse Kit so loud?

Embarrassed, Ember realized that it was her own shame about the entire situation making it seem as if Nurse Kit was yelling. In fact, the other woman was practically whispering. Perception was a hell of a thing.

"Guess the gossip mill is going crazy."

"Bonkers."

"I still don't understand how you recognized me."

Now it was Nurse Kit's turn to look slightly uncomfortable as she stared at Ember's complexion while her tongue tried to shovel out words from the back of her throat. Ember quickly understood the older woman's implication.

"It also makes it pretty obvious seeing as I'm the only Latina for miles."

"Just a few miles," The skin near Nurse Kit's eyes pinched as a good-natured mirth emanated from her aged face.

"It's okay. I get it. I'm the only Latina for miles and I've managed to dive headfirst into the center of a criminal investigation. Probably the worst thing that I could have done in a town petrified of the unknown. I should be fired as the unwilling cultural ambassador."

"Probably. To be fair, you're only stuck in the position because you're different. In places like this, people tend to fear that change, especially when they don't know any better."

An awkward pause passed over the duo. Kids screamed and sprinted from one side of the hall to the other. Ember took a few steps to the left as a hollering toddler sprinted down the hall.

"I guess this place is too small to have a children's wing," Ember observed.

"We did. Now, it's under renovation. We had a bit of a pest problem on that side of the building. Ants. Hopefully we will be back to normal before the end of the year."

"That's almost ten months from now. I think that's a safe bet."

Nurse Kit leaned against the wall and acted as if the center of the bustling hallway was her home. She clucked her tongue in the back of her throat, "Hopefully, time is a funny thing. A lot can happen in a few days and at the same time nothing can change in the span of a few years."

"Perspective."

Nurse Kit agreed, "Perspective."

Ember realized that this was probably the opening that she had been looking for. She nervously licked her lower lip before she began, "Speaking of perspective. You've probably seen everything while working here. Tons of babies now turned into adults and a good amount of loss."

"Yes, hospitals see the full circle. It's humbling, but I appreciate how personal it is within a smaller hospital. I really get to know my patients and it's great to see them out and about from time to time."

Ember nodded her head. She decided to be blunt, "Did you know the women?"

Nurse Kit sighed and her proud shoulders slumped down about an inch. The question seemed to suck the life out of her. She instantly appeared much older as if time had somehow caught her by surprise and stolen several years.

"Yes, I knew them very well. Very sweet women. I honestly would even venture to call them girls. So young."

Ember nodded and hedged, "Do you know if they had anything in common like a disease? Maybe similar activities?"

"I can't disclose personal information about patients."

"They're not patients, not anymore," Ember winced at the sound of her own voice. Why the hell would she say something so harsh? Idiota.

"You're right," Nurse Kit's attention moved to something in the distance. A memory that Ember couldn't see.

Ember walked a few steps closer and pressed her hands together in a begging motion, "Please. I want to fix this. No one else needs to die. Help me have a fighting chance at making this right."

An expression flashed across Nurs Kit's gaze, but it happened so quickly that Ember didn't have time to interpret it. The action was an easily dismissable fluke.

"I can't give away information," Nurse Kit's tone sounded contemplative and it gave Ember hope.

She needed to find the right words to persuade Nurse Kit to help her out. Ember looked over to the desk placed in the middle of the hall. It was obviously one of the nurse's stations. Behind the desk, Ember noticed a pile of wayward boxes. Black marker sloppily etched across the side indicated that they were decorations for one of the Valentine's Day floats.

"Do you need help decorating?"

"No, I need help cutting," Nurse Kit narrowed her eyes at the stack of unwelcomed boxes.

"What?"

Nurse Kit hastened to explain, "My granddaughter won the high school's Heart Stopper of the Year Award. The float is supposed to be covered with red and pink paper hearts. I got roped into helping and I don't really have time."

"Makes sense. What if I helped out with the hearts? I can do a box or two."

Nurse Kit sized Ember up. She folded her arms over her chest and slowly nodded her head. Her gaze seemed to imply that she was willing to help Ember out, "They were all young and vibrant. Each one of them had dreams. Wanted a future. Envisioned more. I don't believe that they had any common diseases or similarities beyond that. I'm sorry."

Nurse Kit paused and then gave a cursory glance around the hall before she continued, "Bring back the hearts when I'm off work and maybe we can talk again."

Damn. That wasn't nearly as helpful as Ember had hoped. She looked at Nurse Kit and noticed the sincerity in her features. The woman didn't have a reason to lie. Did she?

"Thank you, I'll be around if my friend needs me."

Instead of replying, Nurse Kit simply nodded her head and walked away. The conversation ended as abruptly as it had begun.

Ember walked up the stairs and sat down in the tiny hospital cafeteria. She needed a moment to think. The tuna sandwich that she had plucked from the grab-and-go section appeared revolting, but she knew that she'd need to eat. It was almost noon. She looked up and noticed a couple near the back of the room eating the tuna sandwiches. They still looked alive. Maybe the potato salad would have been the safer bet?

It didn't matter. Ember rewrapped the sandwich and decided to take it with her. Food poisoning was pretty low on her list of worries. If she did get sick then at least she was already at the hospital.

    Ember entered the empty elevator. She pressed the lobby button and paused. A button below the lobby appeared unmarked. The building was relatively compact in length. It had been built upwards to avoid being flooded when the lake overflowed after a heavy rain. The unmarked button haunted Ember. She knew what lurked inside of the deceptively unmarked belly of the hospital. The morgue was hidden in plain sight.

    The elevator suddenly felt too small. Ember stared at the buttons and watched with bated breath as the elevator moved. It was going too far down. She was headed for the ground. A strangled sob wrenched its way out of the back of Ember's throat as the lights went out and the elevator fell lower and lower. It descended on a path to nothingness.

Chapter 31

"That wasn't on my bingo card for today."

Ember sped out the front doors of the hospital as if the ends of her long dark hair were on fire. She had had enough excitement for the day. The elevator had malfunctioned and managed to trap her between the morgue and lobby for several minutes before a technician had sorted out the problem and set her free.

Luckily, Ember didn't consider herself claustrophobic. Otherwise, she was convinced that it would have been an absolute nightmare. She headed away from the building, lost in thought.

A light layer of fog swirled around her ankles as she walked closer to the cemetery. She figured that the dead would be an easier crowd to socialize with. Tombstones lined the walk. Some names were too worn to properly discern. The cemetery held the last names of the very first settlers of Ashburn. It seemed unimaginable that people were able to live and die in the same place. Ember wondered what it would be like to grow up in a previously quiet town, settle down, grow old, and eventually pass on. Who was she to judge someone's quality of life? Was her life any better?

"Stop being so introspective. It's depressing as hell," Ember looked down and stepped a little to the side. She didn't want to trample the small orange flowers that were blossoming near the graves. The bright pop of color offered the slightest bit of levity to the bleak location.

Eventually, Ember spotted a concrete bench nestled on the top of a small hill. She closed the distance and settled onto the top. It was nice to have such an elevated vantage point. The ground was so incredibly flat that the added height allowed Ember the chance to glimpse Main Street. She could see the heart of the town's life while directly positioned within the womb of death.

A loud caw grabbed Ember's attention. She instantly recognized the sound. Black wings flapped in front of Ember's vision as one of her friends came to sit on the opposite side of the bench.

Ember placed her elbow against the back of the bench and asked, "Qué estás haciendo aquí?"

She angled her head so that she could catch the massive bird's gaze. Of course, that proved virtually impossible as the crow kept shifting his attention around the graveyard.

The bird was impressively sized and had gleaming feathers. He was an animal in his prime. Wild and calculating. Ember sighed, "You found me, Brutus. Glad you decided to join. It's been a shit day and it's not even time for lunch. Did you get into any trouble this morning?"

Her question was greeted with the sound of tapping as Brutus nudged his beak along the side of the roughened bench. The aggressive action momentarily alarmed Ember. She was afraid that Brutus was about to harm his beak in one of his classic displays of destruction.

Ember reached out a hand and patted the feathers on the side of the massive bird's neck. Instead of snapping at her or clipping her two fingers, the animal simply crooned.

"You're okay. Would you like some food?"

The crow shook out its feathers and then danced closer to Ember's extended arm. Clearly, he thought that she had a snack. He wasn't wrong.

Ember pawed around in her bag and retrieved the tuna sandwich that she had just purchased from the hospital cafeteria. The unexpected elevator ride had managed to extinguish the previous flames of hunger that had licked around her belly.

"Here."

She tore up one half of the sandwich and held out her hand. Slowly, Brutus crept closer. He swiftly plucked the sandwich from Ember's hands and then retreated back to his spot on the bench. He made quick work of the meal and left a mess of bread in his wake.

Brutus shook out his feathers and lowered his head. A small clank brought Ember's attention to the bottom of the bench. She murmured, "What did you drop, Brutus?"

"Oh, no. Brutus, I can't accept this. Where did you get this?"

Ember held the glittering chess piece up in the air. The crystal chess piece was shaped like a queen. She tilted the piece to the side and watched as beams of light danced along the reflective surface, "It clearly belongs to a sophisticated chess set."

Brutus blinked up at her with dark eyes. He didn't give a damn.

"You know, they say that chess is all about protecting the king. Even so, the queen is the piece that holds the most power."

Ember absently reached out and scratched underneath Brutus's chin, "You have some courage, bird."

As if Brutus knew exactly what she was saying, he bellowed loudly and pecked around the violent crime scene of discarded sandwich bits. Within seconds, he ate all of his previously discarded crumbs.

"I know, Brutus. You speak English better than I do. It's not something I'm proud of. Maybe one day the language will come easier to me."

Ember remembered all of the times in school when she had struggled to pronounce English words. At first, the memories were hard to recall like pulling out old Christmas decorations from the back of a closet. One by one, the memories returned. She recalled how cruel the other kids had been to her when she had desperately tried to learn how to read. She had been in first grade so they all had been learning how to read, but still.

Ember's accent had made her an excellent target for bullying. She hated speaking in class. It had made her stomach twist in anxiety. The memories managed to dampen Ember's already gloomy mood. She looked over at Brutus and sighed, "Once this investigation is over, I'm buying you and the rest of the crows the best and biggest bag of seeds."

Ember fed the last chunks of tuna to her friend and wiped her hands on a thin one-ply napkin. She wrinkled her nose as the scent of fish lingered on her fingers.

"Yuck."

She stood from the bench and Brutus hopped a few paces back. He cawed in protest and Ember laughed, "You're right. Who's going to miss a random chess piece?"

Ember's steps faltered down the hill. That was it. She had been playing checkers instead of chess. Finally, Ember understood that she needed to go back to the very beginning and look at everything from a distance. This wasn't a situation where she could be reactive or impulsive. She needed to be calm and calculated.

Decided, Ember realized that she needed to piece together both the past and the present. Maybe, there were more than a few clues hidden in time. Forgotten clues just waiting for an opportunity to foretell the future.

The cold nipped along Ember's wrists as she called out, "You're a genius, Brutus!"

Chapter 32

The look slapped across Ray's face spoke volumes about his anger. He tapped the fingers on his right arm against the side of his temporary cast.

"Where were you? How can I keep you safe if you don't keep still?"

Ember rolled her eyes as she entered Ray's room and helped him stand from the bed. He had been given the green light to leave. The doctor had given Ray the good news only a few minutes after Ember had returned from her graveyard adventure. Perfect timing.

"How can you protect me from a hospital bed?"

Ember quickly bit down on her lower lip. The statement wasn't fair. She added in a much softer tone, "You're in here because of me. If you were smart then you'd be happy when I'm far away."

Ray turned rigid. The hand that he had placed on Ember's shoulder for support flexed just enough so that his fingers roughly pressed into her skin. He stopped moving. Ember stumbled as she was met with a seemingly immovable wall. Damn, Ray really knew how to throw around his weight. She yanked on his arm again, but he didn't budge. They were trapped until Ray decided to move.

The room filled with a tense silence. Ember knew that Ray was mulling over her words. It was only a matter of time before he realized that he was standing next to a ticking time bomb. He would be better off overseeing the case from the safety of the Sheriff's Department.

"Don't you ever say such foul garbage to me, again. Are we clear, Ember?"

The fury behind Ray's words momentarily threw Ember for a loop. She tilted her head to the side so that she could see the emotions swirling behind Ray's gaze. His eyes were dark as he gritted out, "You're not the problem, Ember. Whoever is going around town and murdering women wants you to think that you're the problem. If you isolate yourself then you'll be this madman's easiest target, yet."

Ember didn't trust her voice so she simply nodded her head. The gesture clearly didn't satisfy Ray as he repeated,

"Do I make myself clear?"

"Yes."

"Good. Help me get out of here."

"Sure. Can you grab that bag with your good arm, Ray?"

Ray noticed the large grocery bag that Ember had carried into the room. Pink and red paper poked out from the top. It was stuffed with at least a few hundred pieces of construction paper. He inclined his head to the side and asked, "What's that?"

"A favor."

Chapter 33

"What does cutting paper hearts have to do with solving the case of a serial killer?"

"Nothing, maybe everything."

Ray was propped in the center of the bed. Donna had been more than accommodating. The older woman allowed Ember and Ray to stay another night for free.

Ember walked over and gave him another bottle of water. She sat down on the edge of the bed and tapped the side of his foot. She noticed the perplexed look on Ray's face and continued, "I have a hunch. I need to find out what Nurse Kit knows about the murdered women. I have a feeling that she was holding back. I plan to ask her again once we've finished all of the hearts."

"That's a very liberal use of the word we. Why does she need all of these brightly colored hearts? Is she hosting a Valentine's Day party?"

Ember reached into the bags of arts and crafts supplies that she had purchased on their way back to the inn. She pulled out a blank board and propped it against the desk. She turned back to Ray and explained, "No. The town hosts an annual Valentine's Day Parade. It's a pretty big deal. We have two days to make all of the hearts in that bag. I'm giving them to Nurse Kit during the parade."

She inclined her head, "You craft the hearts and I'll make the murder board."

"Murder board," Ray mumbled. His lap was littered with bright scraps of colored paper. He looked ridiculous.

Ember explained, "It's like a vision board, but it's all about murder."

Ray shook his head as he jokingly replied, "That was my second guess."

"I can't believe Valentine's Day is already here."

"Not a fan of public displays of affection?"

"Close. The older I get, the faster time seems to pass. Some memories and events are like buoys, floating over the sea of my life. Floating and helping me to remember where I've been. Some of my mental buoys are painful. Time keeps pouring in and filling me with memories. I feel like we all started with memories that were the same size as puddles and then time expands our meaning and our little puddles. It gives us an entire ocean of memories if we're lucky enough to live a long life. The funny thing is that some memories in that ocean aren't real. They're more what we felt or would like to remember than the actual event. Still, it's all mixed and jumbled together. Like the mysteries lurking in the ocean."

Ray gave Ember an inquisitive look as she stared off into the distance. Eventually he teased, "Have you ever thought about starting a podcast?"

"Callate," Ember waved her hand in the air and continued, "I always get weirdly sentimental around this time of year. Ignore me. Let's focus on building this murder board."

"Oh, no. You're not getting out of this so easily. Why are you so sentimental?"

"The day after Valentine's Day is a sensitive day for me."

Ray seemed to weigh his words. Instead of prying, he stated, "That's close."

"Not much to celebrate this year," Ember's voice softened. She opened a file and began to thumb over details from the decades-old cold cases.

"You're still here. That's something to celebrate," Ray resumed cutting out paper hearts. He was slowly getting the hang of the process. He placed two pieces of paper together in order to cut out two hearts at once. His focus might have remained on his hands, but Ember knew that he was silently mulling over her words.

Ember hated how he seemed to know when she was lying. She wondered if that was what made a truly good detective. The ability to smell out another person's bullshit. It seemed possible.

"Let me focus on making this murder board," Ember cleared her throat as she turned around and searched for a task demanding enough to distract herself.

"Sure. Don't mind me. I'll be carefully cutting out tiny hearts because it's definitely the difference between life and death."

"Sarcasm won't help you cut out tiny paper hearts any faster."

"True, but it makes me feel better."

Chapter 34

The board was covered in multicolored yarn. It looked like a convoluted spider's web with neon green string interspersed between vibrant reds and calming blues. Ember rubbed her eyes as she took a step back. She had put all of the information about the previous cold cases onto the murder board.

Three women were murdered in the 90s without so much as a whisper of a connection. Ember stared at the details that pertained to each woman. Three bright smiles. Three bright futures. All permanently extinguished without cause. The bright lively faces sharply contrasted the evidence and details surrounding their deaths.

All women looked different. Their hair colors ranged from red, black, and blonde. Their features were varied, but mostly caucasian. Of course, Ember was willing to bet that had to do with the fact most women tended to be caucasian in the area.

However, they were all relatively young. Ember realized that none of them had been older than 35 years of age. There had to be something else. A bigger connection.

She needed to start a board about the most recent deaths in order to look for connections. It was somewhere.

Ember was sure that she was just looking in the wrong place. Her eyes moved from one section of the board to the next.

Three women over the span of three years had all been murdered in a similar fashion. The authorities had supposedly caught the killer, but the final murder had happened while the key suspect had been under arrest. So much for that lead.

Ember rubbed her eyes with the back of her palms as frustration settled deep into her bones. Where was the connection? Each face seemed to haunt Ember the more that she took in their features.

She sat down and decided to make a second murder board about the two most recent murders. For a moment, Ember considered leaving room for another victim. Instead, she decided that it would be best to completely fill the board. Leaving any empty space felt like inviting another murder.

No thanks.

Ember frowned, she realized that the details surrounding the location of the last two murders were missing. She looked at the board to the right. It was covered with information about the past. Ember read over the information pertaining to locations of the previous cases.

A cold chill slithered down Ember's spine. She had an idea about where the two most recent murders had occurred. Well, not exactly.

Ember spoke in a voice that was barely above a whisper. She didn't want to be right, but she had a strong hunch about the repetition. The importance of dredging up the past. She whispered, "The most recent women, were their bodies found near the old candle factory and the Whitmare Bridge?"

Ray stopped fussing with the colored paper. Ember kept her back turned so that she was facing the two boards. Her eyes aimlessly scanned the two surfaces for information. She was practically begging them to speak. However, another part of Ember didn't want to know. She feared what would happen if she was right. A small enough detail to confirm her suspicions.

The bed creaked as Ray shifted. He robotically replied, "I am not permitted to share key details of an ongoing investigation with the public."

"I need to know. You tell me yours and I'll tell you mine, remember?"

"That's not how that is supposed to work, Ember. I need to know everything that you know. You are not permitted to know everything that I know. This is not a two-way street."

"I prefer to beg for forgiveness."

Ember waited. She knew that Ray was weighing his options. He was stuck between upholding the rules of his job and helping Ember solve the case. Two contrasting concepts with the same ultimate goal.

"You don't need to tell me," Ember turned around. She looked deep into Ray's eyes as she emphasized the word tell. Her hint was clear as she continued, "You don't need to tell me if the most recent murders were found in the same locations as the ones from the 90s. To drive home her point, Ember nodded and then shook her head.

"Clever. I can't tell you." Ray followed her lead and then nodded his own head. It was affirmative. Ember's guess was right. She slumped against the wall and added, "Were they moved from a different location?"

"I can't tell you that." Ray once again nodded his head to tell Ember that she was right.

The pulse on the side of her neck thrummed as if she was running a marathon. How many people knew the locations of the original string of murders?

It was a small town and mouths tended to wag. Even if the information wasn't printed in the local papers, it probably wouldn't have been hard to find. Still, it was the first true thread between the past and the present. A true indisputable commonality. Ember realized that there was a strong possibility of a copycat.

Perhaps there was a new murderer in town, hoping to go unnoticed by mimicking the original killer. It was possible. Copycats did happen, especially after high-profile killers.

Even if the Ashburn killer hadn't been famous before, Ember's podcasts had definitely helped skyrocket him into notoriety.

Back to square one. It was a clue without any clear direction. Deep down, Ember refused to just kick it under the rug. She decided to pull on the strings in the hopes of finding more commonalities.

Oddly enough, the realization that she was right didn't excite her like it had in the past. She found no pleasure in realizing that she was right. The previous excitement had turned stale on her tongue. Bitter.

She couldn't believe how foolish she had been. How had she never felt the gravity of the previous deaths that she had talked about on her podcast? She had enjoyed investigating and delving into the cases, but none of them had truly felt real. How many crime scenes and murderous details had she poured over without even a flinch? How had she ever been able to investigate the implosion of a family's universe while feeling nothing?

Ember was rudely aware of the change. Now, all five of these women felt real. She could practically see them coming to eat at Patty's Diner after a long day of work. Ember was no longer dealing with fictional people, she was dealing with ghosts. People that would haunt her in her dreams. Women that deserved better than passing into the unknown before their time.

As if Ray could see the gears in her head turning, Ray pressed, "What have you found?"

Ember tried to keep her tone light, "Besides a headache? Nothing. I need to go feed the birds."

"You'll figure it out. I'll get ready."

"You plan to join?"

Ember's question was met with a look that practically screamed frustration. Ray was definitely coming to watch her feed the crows. She sighed and then flipped the murder boards so that they were facing the wall.

"Why did you do that?"

"I don't want to see their faces when we come back. The boards are too close to the bed. The room is so cramped."

Ray understood what Ember was really trying to say. They had no separation from the case. It was literally in the room with them. Hovering. Waiting.

"I need a favor, Ray."

"That's not good," he hobbled into the bathroom to get changed.

Ember kept her gaze focused on the bed. She noted that Ray hadn't bothered to lock the bathroom door. The familiar click of the pesky door remained absent from the tiny room.

She prodded, "Can you arrange a meeting with the sheriff? First thing in the morning? If he says no then tell him that we will pay for his breakfast if he meets us at the diner. He loves that place."

"What's the catch?"

Ember scuffed her shoe on the carpet as she stalled. She didn't know how to tell Ray that the sheriff hated outsiders. Ember knew that her only shot at getting information would come from meeting the old gunslinger alone. Ray wouldn't be able to breathe down her neck.

Ember circled around the main catch, "Will you loan me some money to cover the sheriff's breakfast?"

Ray chuckled, "Yes, I expected to be on the hook for that bill."

"I'm not in a position to pay. Rent is due the 15th and that's right around the corner. I have just enough for this month, but next month."

Ember suddenly halted the sentence. The implication was clear. Without a job, she'd end up unable to pay for rent the next time around. March was going to be bleak. If she even lived long enough to see it.

Ember pulled her attention back to the current conversation. She asked, "How about you grab a bite to eat across the street while I get him to talk?"

Ray struggled to put on his jacket with one good arm. His movements grew more agitated as he listened to Ember speak. The poor jacket didn't have a chance. A sharp rip groaned in the air as the shoulder of Ray's jacket tore.

"Damn."

"Stop floundering around like a fish. Let me help."

"I can do it, Ember."

"Sure you can, Champ. Now stop moving before you really rip the other shoulder and you have to leave the room looking like you got mugged."

"I'll just tell everyone that you mugged me."

Ember groaned, "Don't do that. Everyone will believe you. I'll just meet with the sheriff alone, okay?"

Ray took a step back, "You still don't trust me? You don't want me around when you talk to the sheriff. Do you know how easy it would be for me to get rid of you, Ember? Do you have any idea how simple it would be for me to get rid of you if I really felt the need?"

He took a step closer with every sentence. Ray stopped when their shoes touched. Ray leaned down as he glared at Ember. His nostrils flared as he tried to drive home their obvious physical differences. He easily had 100 pounds on Ember.

Instead of scooting away, Ember stood on the tips of her toes and called his bluff.

She hissed, "Do you really think it would be a matter of brawn? I would be an idiot to trust you. I am also an idiot for not trusting you. Both options suck because there is a large chance that I'm wrong, either way. So we're clear, I spent my free time learning about murderers and criminal behavior. This might be your job, but I did it for free. I did it for fun."

Ember made sure that Ray heard each and every word before she continued, "When it comes to the sheriff, I know that he won't speak openly if you're around. He hates outsiders and barely even trusts me. The only reason he might tell me what I'm hoping to know is that we were amicable when I worked at the diner. The man has a soft spot for all things Americana."

Ray's stare softened as he took a step back. He scratched the back of his head and mumbled, "Apologies."

Ember shrugged in response. She had half a mind to give him shit, but decided to wait. She wanted to wait until he really pushed her buttons.

The duo headed out and Ember double-checked the lock on their door. She smirked as she walked behind Ray. His jacket looked dumb.

Chapter 35

The diner smelt of grease and burnt coffee. Ember inhaled and sighed in relief. She felt that the diner was somehow a sacred place. A business where people from all backgrounds and walks of life could safely congregate for a meal. A safe watering hole. Mostly, Ember liked it because her stomach was moaning like a massive ballena. A big whale.

She stood up from her seated position and waved as the sheriff entered the diner. He headed back to her corner booth near the window. From the corner of her eye, she noticed the faintest outline of Ray's form as he sat across the street at the Hamburger Happy Hut. Ray's gaze was practically drilling a hole into the side of Ember's head. She tried her best to ignore him. Easier said than done.

Ember firmly shook the sheriff's hand and then slid into one side of the booth. One thing that Ember greatly appreciated about the sheriff was that he always cut to the chase. He had no interest in fake pleasantries. The man never bothered to ask how you were unless he actually gave a damn. It was refreshing. He was the kind of man that would at least shoot you in the face.

"Thanks for meeting me, Sheriff Arthur."

"I've told you to call me Art."

"Art," Ember paused as a waitress ambled over to the table.

"Hey Dolls, what can I get for you?"

Art gestured for Ember to go first, "A black coffee, please."

"Two black coffees," Art clarified as the waitress quickly hurried away. She was likely eager to escape the intense atmosphere that hovered above the table.

When the waitress was out of earshot, Ember began, "I'm in trouble."

"Yes."

Ember sighed and tried a less obvious opening statement, "You probably have the most information about the case. Would you mind telling me what happened two decades ago?"

Ray rubbed the back of his neck as if even generally thinking about the 90s gave him a bad headache. It was possible.

"I thought we had him, but it turns out we were wrong. Now he's back and I can't figure out if your podcast is the reason for his reappearance or just a convenient excuse."

Ember muttered, "I was wondering about that, too."

It was a welcomed perspective. Ember had tentatively considered that she was just an excuse for a much larger plan. If that was true, what was going to happen next? An icy hand gripped the back of Ember's throat. She forced herself to focus on the moment.

"What happened between 1995 and 1998?"

Art's eyes grew distant as he returned back to the past. He tapped a finger on the wooden table, "The end of Ashburn happened. Those women had so much life. We all knew them. How would we be able to place blame on any one person if everyone had access to them? We were all friendly with each person in the town."

"So you thought it was the town's outcast?" Ember noticed the edge of accusation in her tone and bit her lip. She realized that if she annoyed Art then all he had to do was stand up and walk away.

"What was the other option? Pretend that it never happened?"

Sheriff Art's cheeks turned flushed with emotion as his breathing increased. He stopped speaking and grabbed the still-scalding cup of black coffee. Sheriff Art took a long sip.

Perhaps he drank the burning liquid, in a desperate attempt to cleanse the inside of his body from a terrible poison. Perhaps, his time as a sheriff had indeed poisoned him. At some point, maybe the voices of the people that he couldn't save ended up seeping into his bones.

No.

Maybe this particular case was poisoning Ember. Slowly tainting her from the inside. Starting in her chest. The poison pulsed outwards with every steady beat of her heart. Maybe it was already too late. The poison was already too deep.

"What's on your mind, Sheriff Arthur?"

"Art. If I need to correct you again then I'll have to arrest you."

Ember took the comment in stride. It was obvious that the older man wasn't able to explain exactly what was on his mind. The weight was perhaps too heavy to remove all at once. She appreciated his twisted attempt at a joke.

"You remind me of someone, but I can't put my finger on it."

Ember rolled her eyes, "You've said that before, Art. Multiple times. My mom grew up here. Mystery solved. Stop stalling and tell me what you know so that no one else needs to die."

Ar narrowed his eyes as he inspected Ember's features, "Maybe."

Sheriff Art cupped the mug with the palm of his right hand. The innocent action made the cup appear significantly smaller than usual. It was as if the bulking salt-and-pepper-haired man was holding a cup made for a child. Art was older but still capable. A potential bull in a glass shop. He clenched and unclenched his hand around the beverage.

"At first, we had thought that it had been an accident. We had found Hallie crumpled on the side of the bridge. The department had assumed that she had managed to climb out of the water only to drown from the remaining water in her lungs. A fluke. A town tragedy, but nothing more. Of course, Hallie's mom had battled the coroner's ruling from the start."

"Hallie had been the captain of the varsity swim team. She had known better than to swim in the lake alone."

Ember couldn't help it. She interrupted Sheriff Art's train of thought and asked, "Wait, what's so wrong with swimming in the lake alone?"

"You're distracting from the story, Kid. But since you ask, the lake has unpredictable rip currents and whirlpools. The right conditions can drown a person, even if they are a capable swimmer."

Unsure of what to say, Ember simply nodded her head in agreement. She had always thought that the lake appeared pensive, but she had never perceived the true danger lurking within its depths.

"Promise me that you won't go into the water," Sheriff Art's tone was practically begging her to see reason.

Ember simply nodded her head, she didn't have the heart to tell him that the lake was the least attractive body of water that she had ever seen.

"Good. Stop pulling from the subject that you begged me to talk about. Where was I?"

"Hallie," the name stung Ember's tongue. She wanted to keep speaking, but her throat felt tight. She was speaking about a dead woman, but wisps of the woman's life kept rolling around in the back of Ember's mind. She felt like she was stuck watching a bad film. The b-roll that she couldn't scratch from the record. Ember hadn't known Hallie, but she was getting the feeling that in some ways she had. Each day was pulling Ember closer to a faint shadow of the murdered women. She was chasing ghosts in the hope of catching a living threat.

Ember winced but tried to cover it by holding the cup of quickly cooling coffee to her lips. She kept her eyes on Art.

Art was sitting on the opposite side of the diner's booth, but his mind looked a million miles away. He took in a deep breath as if to expel the demons lurking in the corners of his mind.

Art grumbled, "They all deserved better. Each woman had a promising life ahead of them. It was about a month later that we found Sandra. That's when we realized that Hallie wasn't an accident. The old candle factory was about a mile away from the lake. She couldn't walk a mile while drowning in the water in her lungs. What were the odds? We had to dig deeper. The town was crawling with police. Women were leaving work early for safety while every single man with a history of being abusive was investigated."

Ember interjected, "So you never considered that the culprit could be a woman?"

Art's lips thinned in displeasure, "I am all about equality, but in some places, women and men are not equal."

Art noticed Ember's shock and hastily continued, "A woman can aim a gun and kill a person just as well as a man. She can wrangle a cow into a pen just as well as any cowboy. But a woman's strength also comes from how she differs. I'm sure you know this, Ember. According to crime statistics, women are better than men. More than 90% of all homicides in the world are committed by men. At the end of the day, I'd sooner trust a strange woman than a man. I only had one woman murderer in this town. One. Do you know what she did?"

Ember frowned as she struggled to absorb the shift in the conversation. How could she have so deeply misjudged Art? Maybe she had simply painted him as a backward sexist sheriff because that's what she had wanted to believe from the start. She hadn't taken the time to really see him.

She simply shook her head in response to Art's question. Ember didn't trust her voice. She was sure that anything that she said would come out as a squeak.

"She was convicted of murdering her abusive boyfriend. A clear act of self-defense. Apparently, a person has every right to defend themselves from danger unless that person is a woman. Do you know what the jury gave her? She was sentenced to 15 years in prison for attempting to save her own life. It was a damn injustice, I had half a mind to give her a medal. One less rabid dog roaming the town. The way I see it, she did me a favor. You see, juries often give men who violently murder their wives two years in prison. A slap on the wrist for permanently taking a life. So when you ask me why I don't believe that the killer was or is a woman, it's not because I don't believe that women are capable of murder. It's just because I believe we live in a system where men are emboldened to promote destruction."

 Ember prodded, "Isn't that a bit generalist? Unfair?"

 Art took a chug of his coffee and then quipped, "Wasn't this system designed by men? It's a system designed to protect us men from our failures while coddling our atrocities. Women are stuck navigating a system that's eager to punish them for even fighting to exist."

 Ember felt her jaw slacken as her mouth hung open in disbelief. Was Art having a psychotic breakdown? His enlightened take on murder sharply contrasted with his rough-and-tumble demeanor. He looked like any small-town hick, but here he was offering the most insightful and possibly controversial perspective into the American legal system that Ember had ever witnessed.

A sick feeling twisted Ember's gut as she realized that she was a hypocrite on the high horse. She hadn't bothered to even really see the man. Ember had simply painted him as the gringo grouch that had often entered the diner and sipped a pot of hot black coffee all alone. It was starting to make sense why Mayor Smith had such a strong relationship with Sheriff Art.

"So that's why you pulled in that suspect," Ember was starting to understand Sheriff Art's reasoning.

She leaned over the table and eagerly waited for Art's reply. The dark look that crossed his features hinted at his bitterness, but he simply took another gulp of coffee. He glanced over at Ember's cup, but she waved her hand to indicate that she was full. She was already jittery enough.

"I really thought we had him. He was an outsider. He had a history of being rude to women. He lacked empathy and struggled to fit into society. He had all of the signs of a killer. Turns out the bastard was just a run-of-the-mill penniless sexist."

Ember choked on her coffee. Tears pricked the back of her eyes as coffee dribbled down her nose and pooled on the surface of the table. She grabbed a fistful of one-ply napkins and hastily cleaned up the area.

"So you arrested the wrong man?"

"Right. We were just starting to question him when Jessica Spelunky was found. It was obvious that someone had moved her from a first location. We were starting to recognize the signs. Big wigs from the federal government had come into town to help. Jessica didn't fit the pattern. She wasn't a local working woman. We assumed that the killer had made a mistake and crawled into a cave to die. Here's to hoping."

    The noise of the diner was pressing into Ember's senses and giving her a headache. She found it difficult to concentrate. How were people able to sit and laugh while a murderer was turning this town into his personal playground?

    A gravelly voice came from the radio attached to the top of Sheriff Art's shoulder. The disembodied voice called out from the void and requested assistance. Ember didn't mean to pry but the thing was practically screeching compared to the calm ebb and flow of diner conversation. She tilted her head to the side and listened as the voice commanded attention, "Sherriff, please proceed to the old Sheldon farm as soon as possible. Two kids stumbled upon a find and they requested to speak with you."

Chapter 36

"You have a death wish."

"For a detective, it really takes a minute for you to put together clues," Ember winked and shimmied underneath the bars blocking her entrance to the burger joint. It wasn't much of a wall. Ember considered it a gentle suggestion to take the longer route that welcomed customers into the large, mostly desolate parking lot. She wiggled over the wall while Ray observed from a distance.

Instead of entering into an argument, Ray simply shook his head in defeat as he watched Ember make her life harder than necessary. When she had finally crawled over the divider he asked, "Are you finished?"

"For now. I have a lot to share, but first I hope that you didn't order anything from here while you were waiting."

"I grabbed a coffee."

Ember pulled a face and mumbled, "You should be safe."

"What does that mean?"

"I saw pest control checking out the place a few days ago."

"You let me go to a place that had roaches without telling me?"

It was clear that Ray was disgusted by his stiffened posture and clenched jaw. He narrowed his eyes at Ember.

"It slipped my mind! Sorry, the whole crazed murderer on the loose gave me a different list of priorities."

"You're excused."

"You're a big baby."

"What did the sheriff say?"

Now it was Ember's turn to sigh, "He was just getting to the good part when he was needed on a call. Luckily, he gave me a better understanding of the earlier murders. Did you know that they had originally thought that it was a terrible accident? The mom of the first victim had insisted that her daughter hadn't drowned. It wasn't until a second victim was discovered that they realized something was wrong."

"Why does your tone sound somewhat forgiving? I thought you hated Sheriff Art?"

"Maybe I hated the idea of him. It's hard to hate people once you get to know them."

"Fair enough."

Ember's eyes brightened as a sudden understanding flickered to life in the back of her mind. She ran a hand over her disheveled locks, "Wait, maybe that's it. Maybe the killer was in this town all along. Maybe all of the victims were people that he loosely knew. We just need to find out who has been in town for 20 years or recently returned."

"So you're saying that it's not a copycat?"

"No, this feels personal. The way that each woman was discovered seems almost angry. Maybe even eager."

"You're reaching."

"I'm calling it an educated guess."

The duo walked out of the parking lot as Ember slowed her pace. Ray limped along on his injured leg but refused to complain. His gaze held a healthy ounce of excitement as he stared ahead. He kept pace and made only the slightest of winces as the two headed back to the rental car. They needed to check out the locations of the murders.

Ember felt the coffee bubble up from the pit of her belly. She swallowed it back down and turned away from Ray. She shoved her fingers into the confines of her jeans to keep them from shaking. Ray wasn't able to comfortably drive so Ember was stuck with the task.

The drive to the bridge was quiet. A country song flitted into the cabin of the car with just enough volume to be noticeable. It competed for attention against the crunching of gravel as the car swiftly pulled to a stop.

Ember put the car in park and Ray arched an incredulous brow, "That was fast. Are we at the bridge?"

"Small town and a rough road. Yeah, we're at the bridge. It's about a five-minute drive from the center of town. From what I can tell, the area is a hang out for the local high school kids because it gives them room to blow off steam without having to be watched by the rest of the town. The water looks deceptively calm."

"How do you know where the local high schoolers like to hang out?" Ray precariously ambled out of his side of the car.

Ember bit her lower lip but stayed quiet as she watched him hobble out. She didn't want to hurt his pride by rushing over to his door. Besides, he was slower than usual but still capable.

"I can feel you staring at my back. Stop it, Ember."

"No. I'm looking at the back of your jacket because it's covered in dirt."

"Damn. I thought I'd cleaned it off."

"What do you mean?"

"This is my lucky jacket."

Ember muttered, "It can't be that lucky if someone hits your car and then rolls you into a ditch while you're wearing it."

"I heard that!"

"You were meant to!"

The ground sloped at an awkward angle and Ember reached out her hand to steady Ray as they navigated the muddy ground. The afternoon light hit the ground and managed to illuminate some areas better than others. The edge of the water was shrouded in a light layer of mist. The wall of water appeared impenetrable and Ember wondered what was hiding just below its depths. Did she really want to know?

If the last few days had taught her anything, she had begrudgingly realized that some things were better left undiscovered. Damn it.

The ground shifted under Ember's feet and Ray yanked her back. He chuckled as they approached a flatter area and teased, "Who's helping who?"

"I'd like to think it's mutual."

"Always with the sharp remarks."

"A sharp tongue to match a sharp mind."

"Sure, we will go with that."

Ember narrowed her eyes and stopped to stare at the bridge. She had never thought much about the ancient brick structure. Sure, she had thought that it looked as ancient as half of the townspeople, but she had never really thought about the people that had stepped on it before her. Was this really where a young woman had taken her last breath? Had Hallie been moved here post-mortem?

"You're starting to overthink it."

"What?"

"You're getting into your head, Ember. It's tricky to find the middle ground between becoming completely absorbed by a case and feeling absolutely nothing. Most people struggle to find that balance because it's like walking the thinnest tightrope in the world."

Ray paused as he looked at the deceptively calm water and then trailed his gaze back to Ember's paler than usual face. He continued, "You made a podcast dedicated to solving murders. Why?"

That was a loaded question, but Ember decided to try her best. She inhaled and then exhaled her reply, "Because I didn't want them to be forgotten."

"Who?"

"The people that were taken. I also like solving cases and guessing about murders because it also feels like a twisted survival guide. What not to do when alone. Who not to trust. How to overcome an impossible situation. Hell, maybe most of it was just luck. You can plan and plan and still end up taken and six feet under. Still, that doesn't mean that I won't try. I'm rambling. I don't know if what I'm telling you even makes any sense."

Ray angled his body in Ember's direction as he replied, "It makes perfect sense to me."

"Thanks."

Ray cleared his throat, "Why are we here?"

"Ideally, to put the missing puzzle pieces together. I don't know where to start, but this does feel like a good option."

Ember scuttled down the side of the bridge and stood just inches away from the water. She narrowed her eyes and examined the small slope that she had maneuvered down to the edge of the frigid lake. It was steep enough to be cumbersome when fully capable, but when drowning? The odds of someone actually scrambling up the steep and relatively muddy area sounded impossible. What were the odds of someone managing to climb up when tired? When drowning? Ember now understood why so many kids had always tried to climb up from the other side of the lake. This area appeared nearly impenetrable.

"Stuck?" Ray tilted his head to the side as he peered down at Ember. She shook her head and called back, "No. I really doubt that Hallie drowned here. I think that she was moved from a second location. This looks impossible to climb."

"Keep in mind that the terrain several years ago was likely a little different. Still, I believe you."

"Do you see anything near the bridge?"

At Ember's request, Ray began to walk across the bridge. He was clearly a man on a mission to find something out of the ordinary. It was a shot in the dark after so many years. No, worse. A shot in the dark had better odds. These odds felt negative.

Mud squelched underneath Ember's palm as she struggled to climb up the steep embankment. She made a face, clearly displeased with the state of things. Ember looked around and spotted a nearly hidden rope. One side of the rope was staked into the ground. It coiled several times like a snake. Ember couldn't exactly use the rope to climb up, but it would be helpful if she ever needed to get pulled back to shore. Not that she'd ever get into the water.

Ember tried to get up the embankment and groaned, "This is disgusting. If my abuela could see me now. She'd be rolling in her grave, telling me that I'm participating in some white people shit."

Ray's head appeared over the side of the bridge as he yelled, "Ember, stop rolling around in the mud. Come up. I found something."

"Screw it," Ember dug her fingers deeper into the mud for leverage. She willfully wrestled with the filth so that she could escape her accidental prison.

Chapter 37

"What are the odds that this belonged to her?"

"You can say her name, Ray. She deserves to live on," Ember shuffled her feet in discomfort as she stared at the small metallic object in the center of Ray's palm.

"You're right. Do you think that this belonged to Hallie?"

"Possibly. Sheriff Art had mentioned that she had been the captain of her swim team."

"What does the high school swim team have to do with this little metal butterfly?"

Ember rolled her eyes as she gingerly took the object out of Ray's grasp. She held it up so that the item reflected against the bright sunlight. Ember risked a sideways glance at Ray's features as she explained, "It's not a butterfly. Look again. Part of it is missing. It's a silver swan. The head is gone. Look at the ridges on the left side. See? They're wings"

"Yeah, I see, but I still don't understand what that has to do with the high school swim team."

"The swan is the high school's mascot. I know it's not very intimidating. Don't look at me, I didn't pick it."

Ray chuckled, "I wasn't going to blame you, but now you're starting to look pretty guilty."

"Shut up. Do you think it could be a swan?"

"Yeah, I do. Help me put it into this bag so we can collect it for evidence."

Ember was about to place it in the outstretched plastic bag, but stopped short.

Ray frowned, "What's wrong?"

"Don't put it in evidence."

"If it's evidence then it needs to be collected and properly documented, Ember. I can't just hold off until you are able to make another podcast episode about it."

Ember recoiled as if Ray had slapped her in the face. Ray's offhand comment had stung. She had thought that they were getting along, but clearly it had all been just for show. He still only saw her as a nuisance. A potential suspect turned into a vulnerable pest.

Spit flew from Ember's lips as she hissed, "I'm willing to bet that the evidence room at the station is compromised. We both saw how pages were torn out from the older reports. This needs to be kept safe to build a strong case. It can't be put into an evidence room where the killer or the killer's friends have access. Of course, what would I know about this case? I'm just the dumbass that reopened this can of worms in the first place."

Anger boiled Ember's blood as she stepped away from Ray. His jaw was clenched shut as a vein pulsed along the side of his face. He stayed quiet as Ember quickly stalked away.

The metallic object was firmly pressed into the center of her palm. The sharp broken edges of the pin roughly rubbed against Ember's hand. She simply tightened her grip.

Ember tossed the car keys onto the hood of their rental. She wanted to make Ray walk home, but decided that would be a step too cruel. Maybe next time, she mused. She'd do the walking.

Ember's feet crunched over the gravel as Ray yelled at her to stay put. No way. She was perfectly capable of walking back to the stupid inn without the help of someone who was convinced that she was a self-interested lunatic. Ember blinked back tears. She couldn't exactly tell if they were caused by fury or disappointment. The two emotions battled for dominance as Ember trekked along the side of the road.

Chapter 38

"How could you be so impulsive?"

The mud splattered rental car rolled to a stop only a few feet away from Ember. It hadn't taken long for Ray to find her. The engine blew fumes into the crisp air. If this was a cartoon, Ember would bet money that steam would also be spewing from Ray's ears. He was pissed.

"I'm taking a walk."

The car inched forward and kept pace with Ember's strides. Ray kept the car directly aligned with Ember so that he could continue chiding her from a distance. He continued, "You don't get to walk away when you're mad at me."

"Why not?" Ember stopped walking and flung her arms up into the air in frustration. She pointed a finger at Ray and continued, "Why does it matter to you?"

"Damn it," The car screeched to a halt as Ray put the car into park and hobbled out of the driver's side. His sure strides momentarily halted Ember's angry rant.

Suddenly, the world turned upside down as a firm shoulder pressed against Ember's belly. She blanched, "Did you just toss me over your shoulder?"

"Nothing gets away from you, Champ."

For a moment, Ember considered kicking Ray, but then she realized that he had already suffered one car accident. Causing him more pain wasn't going to make anything better. She was mad, but not angry enough to be cruel.

Ray opened the passenger side door with one arm and tossed Ember into the seat with the other. He kept his gaze on Ember and instructed, "Seat belt."

Ember kept her eyes on Ray as her fingers reached across her lap to buckle the seat belt. It clicked into place.

"Good girl."

"Pendejo."

"I'm going to take that as a compliment," Ray closed the passenger door and hobbled around to the driver's seat. His breathing had managed to even out as if the rage that had previously built within his chest had managed to suddenly melt away.

"It wasn't meant as one!"

Ember sunk down into the seat and petulantly folded her arms. The car roared to life as Ray took it out of park. He signaled back onto the road as his hands mercilessly gripped the steering wheel.

"Why did you come looking for me?"

"I'll never leave you unprotected. Look, you can hate me all you want, but do it from somewhere that I can still protect you. I can't risk you getting hurt. Next time just slap me in the face."

"That's a violent request."

"Maybe, but if you need to blow off steam and it keeps you from running away then I'll take it. Space is no longer a luxury that you have. I know that I'm not your favorite person and I'm sorry for acting like a dick, but you're stuck with me."

"Apology not accepted."

"That's fine. You can be perfectly angry at me. Just do it where I can keep an eye on you."

"Bossy."

"Want to grab lunch before heading back to the inn?"

Ember held the broken swan between her fingers. A small smile graced her lips. Unwilling to give in so easily, she muttered a carefully practiced, "Sure."

"Let's grab burgers that don't include any vermin."

Ember gave a small shrug, but she felt her limbs slowly relax as she settled into the embrace of the warm car.

Chapter 39

"Happy early birthday, Ember!"

The greeting was out before Ember had any chance of keeping it silent. She internally winced once she noticed Ray's observant reaction. He was only a few inches away and had easily noticed the friendly greeting. The sentence made Ember feel like she was breaking out into hives.

Donna had let the cat out of the bag. Ember smiled at the kind older woman, but it barely reached her eyes.

She plucked at the strings of her worn jacket and mumbled, "Thank you."

"Do you have any plans this year, Sweetheart?"

Ember winced, but managed to keep her face relatively passive as she explained, "No. I try to avoid celebrating my birthday."

Donna balked, "What! Every birthday should be celebrated to the fullest. When you get to my age, you'll learn that each year shouldn't be taken for granted."

"You're right, Donna. Maybe I'll do something," Ember's empty words were a desperate attempt to escape the uncomfortable topic. She awkwardly shuffled to the side, eager to end the conversation. Ember tried to creep closer to the direction of the exit, anything to escape the well-intended question.

Ray stepped closer and gave Donna a friendly pat on the arm, "We will figure something out."

Donna chimed in, "What about Valentine's Day? At least come to the parade. It's what we do best."

Ember looked back at Donna as she hurried away from the check-in desk. She absently waved her hand in the air and called, "Yes, we already promised Nurse Kit that we'd go. Can't wait to get the show on the road."

Her words were backed by several layers of meaning. Mostly, Ember really wanted to pass the mushy gushy corporate holiday with as little fanfare as possible. Secondly, she desperately wanted to avoid anything and everything related to her birthday, at all costs. Hopefully, getting rid of the overwhelming amount of paper hearts that littered the floor of their room would be a good place to start.

Wait.

Their? Ember scratched the side of her neck in irritation. It was only a temporary arrangement.

"Why do you hate your birthday?"

Ray had one hand casually shoved into his front pocket. He looked ahead, but Ember knew that she had his full attention.

Ember sighed, "It's hard to enjoy something that's wrapped in so many negative memories."

"Negative memories?"

"Well, not memories, more like stories," Ember wasn't exactly willing to volunteer more information than absolutely necessary. Unfortunately, Ray was accustomed to poking and prodding around to find the truth.

He pried, "What do you mean story?"

Ember caved, "Screw it. You asked. My mom told me that my dad left her on Valentine's Day. He left the day before my third birthday. I'm pretty sure she died of a broken heart about a year later. It's not a pretty romance story. She died almost two decades ago, on my birthday. It's hard to remember her."

"I didn't know."

Ember shrugged, "It's fine. I didn't tell you."

"Fair. Do you want to celebrate your birthday?"

The question momentarily caught Ember by surprise. Did she want to celebrate? How many times had she told herself that birthdays were silly while she was growing up? Of course, her grandma had also helped to convince Ember of the notion. It was a tad sick to want to celebrate your granddaughter's birthday on the anniversary of your only child's death.

Ember's grandmother had done an amazing job. More than expected. Above and beyond. But somehow, a small part of Ember wondered what it would feel like to openly celebrate her birthday without feeling guilty.

"Not sure," Ember continued, "It's probably one of those things where you won't know until you try."

Ray nodded his head in agreement. He ran a hand through his dark hair and awkwardly unlocked the door to their shared room.

Ember mumbled a thanks and walked into the confined space. She sat on the corner of the bed as a small smile played along the edges of her lips. She teased, "Do you know what time it is?"

Ray groaned, "We just fed the damn birds."

"Yesterday."

"It feels like these balls of feathers call the shots."

"They're my best and only friends."

Ray quipped, "Not only."

Silence enveloped the room as Ember stared at Ray. She didn't dare to move from her seated position. Instead, she whispered, "Be nice to them."

"Fine. We visit the chickens and then we can get ready for tomorrow."

"I hate to tell you detective, but we're not going into battle. It's just a simple parade."

Ray gave a partial shrug, "Expect the unexpected."

Ember rolled her eyes, "You watch too much TV."

"You listen to too many podcasts."

That was true. Ember decided to hold in her wayward remarks.

Ember slowly stood and stretched her back. Her stiff joints groaned in protest. She looked over her shoulder at Ray and grinned, "Fair enough."

Chapter 40

Shades of passionate red and vibrant pink danced around the street. Children sprinted down Main Street. Many of their little faces were painted to resemble hearts. Adults donned heart-shaped headbands and wore muted shades of red, pink, and white to adhere to the festive theme. The parade was set to begin in less than a few hours. Parents were feverishly placing the finishing touches on elaborately decorated floats while their kids scurried around the street and played tag.

The scene felt so oddly wholesome that a newcomer would have no idea of the carnage that had occurred only a few days before. The joyous atmosphere almost felt disingenuous. How were people supposed to celebrate in droves while a murderer was on the prowl?

A child brushed along Ember's thigh and pulled her out of her dreary musings. A high-pitched voice drifted along the wind and called, "Sorry!"

For a moment, Ember contemplated yelling back a response, but the kid had sprinted away so quickly that only a blur of hair could be seen. Laughter rang out from every corner and the hairs on the back of Ember's neck bristled in protest. Apparently, the overwhelmingly celebratory mood had failed to put her mind at ease.

Ember hadn't bothered to dress up. In fact, her dark jeans and white top reminded her of her short times spent as a waitress. She tugged along a box filled to the brim with cut-out paper hearts. Her fingers curled more tightly around the items as she walked in Nurse Kit's general direction.

"Hi! You're late," A simple remark. Nurse Kit strode over as two kids clamored near the side of the float. It was designed to look like two swans embracing. The birds were angled so that their necks formed the shape of a heart.

Upon closer inspection, Ember asked, "How many dozens of white roses did that take?"

Nurse Kit followed Ember's gaze and grumbled, "Enough. The plan had sounded festive and perhaps a little camp. Now, all I'm seeing is dollar signs. Luckily, the float expenses are being covered by the school."

The sentence seemed fair enough. It was common practice for many businesses centrally located within town to create a float. The floats were often obnoxiously decorated with elaborate designs thanks to a crowd of overly excited high schoolers. Ember looked over at the side panel of the float and noticed the name of the high school proudly scrawled along a silver plaque.

"Is the plaque made from real silver?"

Ember nudged her head in the direction of the sign. The plaque shone brightly in the pleasant early morning sun.

In response, Nurse Kit simply rolled her eyes and muttered, "I suppose that you should know a little bit more about this float."

Ember frowned, "Excuse me?"

"Yes, it's real silver. The actual silver adds a nice touch of presence and decorum. Now let me make good on my side of our deal."

"That's one way to call it even," Ember held out the box of paper hearts and began to place the crafted items along the bottom of the rose petal swans. The paper hearts were supposed to make it look as if the birds were somehow sitting on a nest of hearts.

Nurse Kit began, "The town rarely came together. For a place with so few neighbors, it often felt isolated. As you know, the next nearest town is several miles away. Our parade was inspired by a neighboring Christmas Parade. Of course, we couldn't outright steal the idea, but Ashburn's board decided to do something similar. We needed a reason to bring people together to celebrate. You know, to get people's minds off things."

Ember placed a large red heart near the tail of one of the extraordinarily large swans. She grabbed another red heart, but Nurse Kit simply plucked it from her hands and muttered, "Pink heart next. You're putting too much of the same color together. It's supposed to look unintentional."

"Let me guess, methodically random," Ember arched a brow at Nurse Kit, but did as instructed. She continued to grab randomly colored hearts as she walked around the literal love nest. If Ember hadn't witnessed it with her own eyes, she would have never believed that Nurse Kit was capable of decorating something so absolutely sappy.

She nudged, "You were saying."

"Right, the parade began about twenty-five years ago. It's about the same age as you. It was created the year after the final murder."

Ember couldn't help herself, she asked, "Why?"

Nurse Kit fixed her with a withering glare that dared her to interrupt again. The older woman placed a heart into the nest without breaking eye contact before she continued, "We needed a reason to come together and move on. It was a way to lift everyone's spirits. Besides, I needed the distraction. The event offered an opportunity to place my focus elsewhere. It worked. Today, this event helps raise over half of our annual funds. People from three towns over often make the drive just to see the floats."

The two fell into a comfortable silence as Ember moved around the float. The pile of hearts was quickly diminishing while the nest continued to grow at an astounding pace. Just a handful of hearts were left unplaced.

Ember tried to focus on the simple and mindless task of placing the paper hearts in an intentionally random position, but something about the conversation had managed to wiggle a memory in the back of her mind loose. She struggled to pull at the mental object that threatened to tumble free with just the slightest push.

Ember gasped, "Intentionally random! It was only designed to look random. Nurse Kit, who is the most powerful woman in town?"

Ember's eyes gleamed with excitement as she looked over at Nurse Kit, she was about to share her hunch with the older woman, but then quickly snapped her mouth shut. It was completely possible that the killer had assistance. Nurse Kit had just freely admitted to being in town during the time of the first murders. The prickly woman had also mentioned that she had also personally required a distraction during that time.

Slowly, Ember released the paper heart in her hand. It fluttered to the bottom of the float.

"Child, what are you doing? What are you rambling about?"

Nurse Kit scolded Ember as she walked closer. Ember instinctively took another step back. Her mind kept wandering to a particular person of interest. A person that at this very moment was likely in danger. The thought alone had Ember's pulse racing in distress.

Nurse Kit might be an accomplice, but she definitely was not working alone. Her presence on the float committee definitely established a solid alibi. She could maneuver around the entire event as she pleased. Her position also gave her access to several guests of honor, including the recently elected mayor. Mayor Hannah Smith.

Ember hopped off the float and awkwardly landed on the concrete. Nurse Kit shouted a furious string of curses and instructions at her back, but Ember couldn't hear a word. She dodged around kids and street vendors as they eagerly set up their carts. Ember needed to find the mayor. She was desperate to find the loose end. The killer's big finale.

She turned in a wide circle and narrowed her eyes at a more isolated part of the street. The vendors and merchants seemed to have temporarily congregated closer to the starting line of the parade. In a few hours, this section of the street would also be full, but at the moment, all Ember could see was the pest control van.

Not a soul was near. Ember struggled to discern what was happening. Distant joyful shouts pulled her attention away from her desperate task. The gravel crunched underneath her weight as she crept closer to the back of the pest control van. She needed a place to hide and the vehicle had unwittingly provided the best coverage. The car managed to shield her from the festive onlookers less than half a block away. She stood still and tried to analyze her surroundings.

Gravel crunched from a distance. Suddenly, a harsh object collided with the side of Ember's face. Shock rendered her momentarily speechless. The searing pain overtook all of her senses. She opened and closed her mouth in a voiceless shout for help.

  A blurry figure stepped into Ember's swaying field of vision. Her eyes blinked slowly as something warm and sticky trickled down the side of her face. Ember gripped the gravel between her palms. A faint voice in the back of her mind whispered that she was about to be taken. A clammy palm reached up to the side of her injured face and touched the dripping liquid. She put her bloodied hand back into the gravel. She hoped against hope that someone would notice her absence. But then again, hope was never something that enjoyed sticking close to her side.

Chapter 41

The scent of intense antiseptic wafted burned the back of Ember's throat. She struggled to open her eyes. Her body begrudgingly cooperated as her lids managed a feeble blink. The room spun as Ember's body remained rooted to the ground. Bile rose in the back of Ember's throat as she struggled to fight off the unpleasant sensation.

Unsuccessful, she twisted to the side and retched the feeble contents of her stomach onto the cold ground. The overwhelming combination of antiseptic and vomit permeated the air. Ember kept her face turned to the side as her stomach attempted another monstrous mutiny against the rest of her body. She dry-heaved and then tried to clean her face. Anger made Ember's blood rush faster through her veins. Of all the times to be kidnapped and bound, it had to be a time when she was violently throwing up her guts. Ember tried once again to move her arms. She realized that she was roughly bound and carelessly discarded on the cold tiled floor.

"I'd offer you some meds for the headache, but I don't trust you alone. Not yet, at least."

Ember looked up and every muscle within her body tensed. She recognized that face. He hulked over her prone form. Ember wished that her hands and legs weren't so tightly bound so that she could inch away from the approaching figure. Ember realized that she had never heard such a cold and calculating tone. How had she missed this?

She fleetingly wondered what else she had missed while stuck in her own little world. Had she missed every clue as they casually stood right in front of her face?

The man that she had least expected lazily strode in her direction. His boots landed only a few inches away from her nose. He then leisurely crouched down and in the most monotone voice imaginable attempted to croon, "It's so good to finally meet you. I can't tell you how many times I've thought of this moment."

Ember opened her mouth to speak, but it felt like she was only capable of making desperate choking sounds. Her chest shook with the motion. Each frenzied heave sent a sharp shooting pain into her skull. It was as if someone had decided to take a sledgehammer to the side of her face. Agony. She bit down on her lip in a desperate attempt to focus on a different source of pain.

In a voice barely above a whisper, Ember asked, "What are you doing?" She felt like the final girl in a horror movie. A large part of her internally cringed at the question. It never seemed to end well when a person in distress asked about their captor;s intentions. Of course, it wasn't exactly like Ember had much to go on.

A dark wicked grin crept along the man's threatening features. He seemed to enjoy watching Ember squirm. Like a deranged child setting ants on fire with a magnifying glass. Eventually, he replied, "What does it look like? I'm spending some long overdue quality time with my daughter."

Chapter 42

"What?"

The ground shifted beneath Ember's bound body. She didn't understand what the lunatic in front of her was trying to say. Clearly, he was deranged for multiple reasons.

Bullshit.

He was spewing bullshit. This man was obviously batshit crazy and if he kept talking, Ember was pretty sure that she'd shit her pants. Maybe a potty mouth did run in the family.

A mirthless chuckle resonated around the dimly lit room. One massive flood lamp illuminated the area. It provided just enough light so that Ember could partly distinguish key features within the room. She gave the space a cursory glance and her heart momentarily sputtered in her chest.

The mayor was bound, gagged, and slouched over in a glass cage located in the farthest corner of the room like a discarded sack of potatoes.

Chapter 43

Ember's hearing grew distant. Her eyes became locked on the crumpled figure only a few feet away. The light barely touched the outline of the mayor's form. She was too far away to tell, but it couldn't be possible. No way. The mayor had to be breathing. It felt as if every cell in Ember's body had screeched to a halt. She couldn't move. She couldn't blink. All she could do was stare.

The beaten figure gave the smallest of groans and Ember's body swiftly snapped back to life. It was something, proof of life. Ember released a shaky breath. How were they going to escape?

"Oh, you've noticed your gift."

Ember's brows pulled together as she attempted to tilt her head enough to the side in order to properly look at the exterminator's features. She desperately tried to recall a name, but realized that most of the people in town had referred to him as the exterminator or pest control guy. She couldn't remember a single time when someone had spoken about him using an actual name. Now, Ember knew why. He had intentionally kept to himself. This mad man had easily navigated the sleepy town using the cloak of an unassuming profession to hide his true nature.

He continued, "I always knew that you'd be back."

The silence was heavy with promise. Ember wanted to find out more, but she knew that asking questions would simply play into his hand. Of course, it wasn't exactly like she had many alternatives. She didn't want to anger him so she decided to indulge him. Ember licked her lower lip and winced, "Back?"

"Linda never told you? My name is Bill. I loved your mother until she betrayed me." It wasn't really a question. His words were a self-satisfied statement. His smug tone sent a shiver of fear down Ember's spine. How did Bill know her mom's name?

As if reading her mind, he added, "We were high school sweethearts. That is until she got corrupted by the city. She ran away to Los Angeles. Can you believe that the bitch tried to hide you from me? What was she thinking?"

Ember could think of a few reasons.

She shut her eyes and desperately tried to recall images of her brave, caring mother. The smell of clean linens and fresh tamales instantly came to mind. The distant memory sent a spark of light into her shattered heart and prevented the bleak nothingness from devouring her whole.

"Did you like my postcard? I figured that I needed to give you an indirect invitation."

Ember swallowed. He was the reason that she had ended up in this town. The realization that she had been manipulated from the start, felt like a punch to the gut.

Fuck this guy. Father was a title that was earned. Ember opened her eyes as a steely confident look entered her gaze. The shift in her emotions visibly threw Bill for a loop. Displeased, his jaw clicked with tension.

Bill reached down and pushed a wayward strand of hair out of Ember's eyes. It took every ounce of self-restraint in Ember's body not to strike out and bite him. Instead, she held painfully still and imagined that her eyes were powerful enough to zap lasers into his head. He appeared pleased that she didn't flinch and continued, "I can't wait to get to know you better. I have so much planned for us."

Ember decided to fish for information. She asked, "How do you plan to bond?"

A deep soulless chuckle reverberated off the walls, "Isn't obvious? We are already bonding. What are the chances that you would stumble across my murders? It's kind of poetic. Like father, like daughter. You already have a knack for the family business, you just don't know it yet. I listened to all of your podcast episodes. You're very creative and pick up on details that the police miss. Your new podcast episodes about me were so insightful. It was like reading a page out of my own diary."

Bill momentarily turned his attention away from Ember as he glanced in the mayor's direction. The mayor had barely moved, but the barely visible rise and fall of the woman's chest provided Ember with the faintest sense of reassurance. If the mayor was breathing then she wasn't dead. That was something.

Ember stopped and looked closer. She narrowed her eyes and realized that something was dripping from the ceiling. It looked as if there was a massive water tank slowly dripping onto the mayor. In fact, it appeared that the mayor was stuck in an area that was sealed with glass. Ember could see the mayor, but couldn't get to her. It took less than a second to know what Bill was doing. He was following Ember's podcast rant and slowly drowning the mayor. Mayor Smith was too wounded to move. If she couldn't lift her head then she'd drown as soon as the glass box filled with only a few inches of water.

Ember bit her already bloodied lower lip to keep from crying out. She knew exactly what Bill was implying. He couldn't make her. Ember decided that she'd rather drown than harm another person. Not that it appeared like she had much of a choice. It looked like she was going to be stuck watching the mayor drown. Ember released a horrified gasp. She was going to be forced to watch the mayor die using a tool from her own imagination.

Maybe Bill was right. Maybe she was just like him.

Bill continued, "I can't wait to tell you everything, Ember. Unfortunately, I don't want to ruin the surprise. Not after spending so much time putting this together for us to enjoy. It will take some time before this starts to get good. I need an alibi so I'll be back."

He stood from his crouched position. The space provided some much needed room for Ember to collect her thoughts. She was going to save the mayor. Whatever it took. The promise instantly locked into place in the back of her mind and solidified itself in the very center of her core.

"I'll be back before midnight, just in time to celebrate your birthday. Oh, and Ember?" Bill paused halfway to the door. He had a wide grin plastered across his features that sent alarm bells whirling in the back of Ember's mind.

Ember lifted her head off the cold ground but remained silent. Not that Bill seemed to mind. He simply continued, "Don't go anywhere."

The door slammed shut and Ember could hear the faint sound of rattling chains from the other side of the exit. Ember listened until the sound of footsteps faded into the distance. She remained on the ground for a few more minutes just to be safe. Once satisfied that he wasn't coming back anytime soon, Ember began to fight against her restraints.

Her mouth reverently caressed the words as she set to work on reclaiming her freedom, "I am my mother's daughter. I am also in deep deep mierda"

Chapter 44

The knots were tight, but after a few painful and nausea-inducing moments, Ember managed to twist onto her belly. The cool floor nipped against her exposed flesh. Ember's shirt had inched above her belly button and the contact with the unforgiving floor sent shivers up and down her spine. She crept along the floor like a worm. Inch by inch. Ember noticed that a brick had fallen from the wall and she hoped that it was sharp enough to break the rope holding her captive. It took several minutes to creep over to the brick and Ember cursed every second of her journey.

She needed to save the mayor. Drops of water fell to the ground and collected in a steadily growing puddle near the center of the glass cell. It was clear that Bill had planned this for years.

Chess.

Ember sped up her approach to the brick. The brick was a dud. Time had worn the corners dull and harmless. She needed to find something sharp. Anything. A light shimmer from across the room drew Ember's attention.

"A rock," Ember was wiggling across the room in an instant. She scraped her chin against the ground in the process, but kept slithering. Her body moved along the ground like a furious snake as she took a direct path to the mayor. A pang of guilt hit her in the chest. Why was she such an ass? She hadn't bothered to check on the mayor. Instead, her first thought had been to search for a way to get free. Maybe she was more like Bill than she wanted to admit.

Shame burned deep within Ember's chest as she approached the slumped woman. She called out, "Hey. Hey, get up! Wake up! Damn it, Delson's is on fire!"

The mayor's eyes flickered open, but then promptly shut. Not even the mention of the mayor's favorite department store catching on fire was enough to fully rouse her from dreamland. Ember tried to look over her companion's body for injuries, but struggled to find any through the class. Ember growled in frustration as her heated breath kept fogging up the glass. The room was poorly lit and only the faintest rays of light managed to filter in from the elevated windows. Bill had removed the mayor's ruby school ring and tossed it to the side. The ring gave Ember an idea. She couldn't reach the mayor, but hopefully she could reach the mayor's discarded ring.

Ember fumbled with the ring and sighed in relief once the corners of the ruby scratched her skin. It was sharp enough that with enough force, she'd be able to get free. Ember yanked the ring down the ropes and apologized, "I'm sorry that I'm abusing your class ring. I don't have money right now to fix it, but I will."

Why the fuck was she apologizing? It wasn't like the mayor could hear her. Ember rolled her eyes at her own stupidity. Her arms burned as she tried to hold the mayor's ring with one hand and hold the knots with the other. Ember tried to be gentle. The last thing that she wanted to do was push too roughly and accidentally break her own fingers.

The sound of subtle sawing combined with Ember's frenzied breathing. She didn't want to waste any time, but it felt unreasonably difficult to break the rope. Ember's motions grew more aggressive as she became increasingly agitated. Each second wasted increased the likelihood that Bill would return. Worse, the puddle within the mayor's glass cage was steadily growing.

The skin along Ember's wrists felt raw, but the pain barely registered. Adrenaline was keeping her focused on the task.

A dull snap happened at the same time that Ember's hands fell to her sides. Pins and needles crawled up her shoulders as her arms dangled lifelessly at her sides. She had no choice but to wait until feeling returned to her appendages.

While momentarily stuck, Ember turned her attention back to the mayor and huffed, "Tell Clarksville University that your ring is sharp as hell. It's practically a hazard."

Sensation returned to Ember's arms in harsh painful bursts. She precariously pushed herself into a standing position. Ember looked down and quickly set to work on freeing her legs. She realized that they were tied with what looked like a simple knot. The knowledge helped to settle some of Ember's dread. She reasoned that she'd at least be able to make the ropes appear tied in the event that Bill returned. She didn't want him to know about her newly acquired advantage.

    A tapping sound from somewhere near the windows had Ember's heart pushing into overdrive.

    Was Bill watching her from a window? Had the psychopath just wanted to watch her squirm before killing her?

    Ember slowly glanced up. Her eyes nervously scanned the tall windows for any sign of a deranged exterminator. Instead, Ember found a sight that managed to bring her back down to her knees.

Chapter 45

A furious crow pecked against the glass. His inky large beak tapped against the surface as he flapped his wings in irritation.

"Hola, Brutus."

The bird released an audible caw as he once again scratched the glass with his sharp talons. Ember narrowed her eyes and realized that Brutus had to be balanced on a relatively stable ledge. From the few times that he had landed on her shoulder, Ember knew that he was a heavy friend. She mentally stored the information away for later as she searched for a way to open the windows. Maybe she could find a way to make a ladder and climb out of the window.

The plan instantly disintegrated into ashes once Ember glanced back at the mayor's still unconscious form. She had little faith in her ability to invent a ladder out of thin air, let alone in carrying another human about two stories into the sky.

"Damn it, where the hell are we? I never noticed such tall windows in town. Where are we? An alternate dimension?"

Ember rubbed a furious hand down her brows and groaned in pain. She needed to focus on solving the problem. The room only had one entrance and she had yet to even give it a try. Maybe she could get out without having to push a bunch of discarded items together. Not that the room had much to begin with.

The door was locked. Sweat dripped down the side of Ember's face as an immense wave of exhaustion threatened to pull her below its murky surface. Ember blinked and attempted to stand. Her early burst of adrenaline was starting to fade. She was in trouble. It was only a matter of time before the pain in her limbs and head decided to return.

She glanced around the room and noticed an odd hooking mechanism near the corner. Ember regretted that she hadn't brought her pocket knife. It was a damn shame.

Without wasting a moment, she sprinted to the corner and grabbed the odd looking stick. It was much heavier than it appeared and her arms tensed from the weight. Ember wobbled over to the wall and hoisted the elongated hook. She could just barely glimpse an odd metallic looking cylinder near the right hand side of the window. Ember angled the hook and felt it lock into place.

She mumbled into the empty room, "It opens the damn window." Her arms felt like they were on fire as she twisted the elongated hook in a circular motion. The window creaked open in protest. It jolted outward and dust fell from the ledge like wayward clumps of snow.

Brutus cawed in protest as he hopped several windows away from the unwelcome movement. He angrily flapped his wings as Ember called in a voice barely above a whisper, "Stop crying, I'm the one trapped."

As if he was able to understand what she was saying, Brutus flapped his wings and swiftly jumped from the ledge. Ember watched as he ascended into the sky and became nothing but a dark speck on the horizon.

Tears pricked the back of her eyes. At least her friend was free. That was something. Ember sniffed and removed the hook from the window.

Ember stared at the hook and wondered if she could use it to plug the water that was threatening to eventually drown the mayor. Ember sped over and realized that the hook was about two feet too short. The hook would never reach. She meticulously returned it back to its place and even made sure that the tiny curve of the handle was facing the same direction as before. Ember didn't want Bill to know that she had managed to get free and explored the room.

She spun around the room as a sense of deep futility nibbled along the edges of her heart. Ember realized that nothing in the room would allow her to reach the window. She was lost to the world.

Chapter 46

The sun shifted its position. It was now just about to disappear from sight. Ember had a sinking feeling that Bill would return any second.

Ember wondered if anyone had even realized that she was missing. Ray had somehow disappeared from sight at the parade. Maybe he assumed that she wanted some time alone. Ember winced as she recalled how emphatically she had refused to get back into the car just the day before. It seemed extremely likely that Ray thought she had simply left to blow off some steam. After all, it was what she did. Instead of confronting her past, Ember had run away from her life in Los Angeles. Memories of her tiny lost family that were too painful to confront. Her madre and abuela lost to time.

Apparently, Ember could run, but she couldn't hide from her family. The irony tasted bitter in the back of her tongue in a similar way to unpleasant cough medicine.

The sick silver lining was that people would notice the mayor's disappearance. Surely, every cop in a 100 mile radius was looking for the mayor. Ember decided to hedge her bets on the people looking for the most powerful woman in town. She would happily be the plus one to that rescue operation.

Chapter 47

A chill entered the air as the room's temperature drastically began to drop. February was notoriously one of the coldest months and Ember knew that she was in trouble. She feared that the cold would eventually enter her bones and rob her of every ounce of strength left inside of her body. Soon, she'd be nothing but a frigid corpse.

Her eyes unwillingly trailed over to the mayor. Ember wondered if her mind was playing a cruel trick on her. It appeared that the other woman's breathing was growing increasingly more shallow. After several more failed attempts to rouse the mayor from her stupor, Ember begrudgingly decided that her best option was to find an escape route. The water was now about an inch high. It was nearing the mayor's face. If the mayor didn't move, she'd start to drown in the quickly forming puddle.

The sound of wings fluttered from above. Ember looked up and her jaw momentarily tensed. Who would take care of her precious friends if she died? She doubted that anyone in town even cared about her lovely birds. Heck, someone in town had even tried to poison them in the past.

"Don't worry. I'm getting out of here. That's a promise," She tilted her head up and spoke her solemn promise to a growing group of feathered onlookers. Apparently, her friends had managed to find her.

    Ember thought darkly to herself that at least they would miss her. The odd thought provided her with a sense of comfort. Maybe it was closure? Frustrated, she yanked on her hair and groaned.

    Furious cawing drew her attention to the opened window. Brutus stood on the ledge as an oddly shiny object hung from his beak. He tilted his head to the side and then dropped the item. It fell for what felt like ages. The minuscule object passed in and out of sight as it tumbled to the floor. The faint clicking sound told Ember that she wasn't losing her mind. She searched the area where she thought that Brutus had dropped the item.

    At first, Ember couldn't see a thing. She was sure that the shiny trinket had been a figment of her imagination. Maybe hypothermia was setting in faster than she had thought and she was already starting to hallucinate.

    She leaned down and began to crawl around on the ground. Her fingers desperately searched over the cracks on the floor and the piles of dirt. She needed to find proof. Her hands shook as they came in contact with the uncomfortable floor.

    A cool metallic surface halted her frenzied search. She swiftly grappled with the object and then pulled it close to her chest. It was real. Brutus had really given her a new trinket. She wasn't losing her mind. For better or for worse, she was in every sense of the word stuck. Stuck in a makeshift prison and trapped in the present moment. Her mind gripped each second in a chokehold. It was as if her mind was afraid of forgetting a single detail of the room.

    Ember glanced down and her lips formed a soundless chuckle. Her friend had just given her the most priceless gift of all. Hope.

Chapter 48

Ember approached the locked door with small, hesitant steps. She knew that the odds were beyond slim. Even as her feet dragged closer to the door, she recognized the pure insanity of her own hope. She was wishing for the impossible.

Brutus had dropped down a thick metal key. The item appeared worn and the item felt several times heavier than normal as it rested in the center of Ember's palm. She approached the door and quickly stopped short. With a sudden jolt, Ember realized that the crack beneath the double-doors was easily large enough to slide the key to the other side. She could push the key out, but what good would that do? She would still be stuck on the wrong side of the door without any way to access the damn lock.

"Think Ember, what would abuela do?"

The question was immediately followed by an answer. Ember knew that her grandma would pray. Abuela had been a devout woman of faith. A faith that Ember had strayed from over the years. Somehow, the woman that Ember had respected and most adored in the entire world had managed to keep her faith even after losing a daughter.

Ember's grip on the key tightened as she tipped her head up to the sky and implored, "Please help. If you are up there then this would be an excellent time for a sign. I know that we're not on great terms, but don't all parents and kids have their moments?"

She scrunched her eyes shut and squeezed the key even more tightly within her grip. The metal teeth pressed so roughly into her skin that small drops of red fell onto the ground.

A loud voice thundered from a distance, "Ember!"

It rang with a commanding urgency that called to the deepest parts of Ember's being. She recognized the concern and anxiety as if it were her own. A small part of her even dared to say that the voice sounded familiar.

She looked up to the massive ceiling and called out, "God?"

Chapter 49

It wasn't God. It was just a stupid, wonderful man. Footsteps pounded down what sounded like a long and empty corridor as a voice frantically screamed out, "Ember?"

Panicked, Ember responded with a swift whisper-yell, "Be quiet! I don't know where he went."

Ray's voice sounded directly next to the door as he prodded, "Who?"

Ember swallowed the thick ball of panic that was quickly growing in the back of her throat. She tried to put into words everything that had happened since the calm early hours of the morning. The comforting worn sheets at the inn felt like a lifetime ago.

How was she supposed to describe the man hell bent on ruining her life? Worse, how was she supposed to speak about the person that she had always envisioned as a hero in her mind?

"Ember?" Ray's voice dipped lower as it took on a concerned quality, "Are you okay?"

"I don't know. The mayor is here with me. She hasn't woken up, but she's still breathing. She's going to drown if we don't get her out. I can't figure out how to break the glass," Ember blinked back a traitorous tear as it threatened to escape.

"I'm not going anywhere, Ember. We're a team. I went looking for you as soon as you disappeared from my side at the parade. At first, I thought that you had left to blow off some steam, but then I realized that not even you are that hard headed."

Ember rolled her eyes, "Thanks for the compliment."

"It wasn't meant as one. Tell me, who did this to you?"

"The pest control man. He says that he knew my mother. Bill says he's my relative."

The sentence wasn't exactly a lie, but it didn't fully convey the truth of the situation or at least Bill's version of the truth.

As if sensing that she was withholding information, Ray paused, he waited for Ember to continue her story.

Instead, Ember spoke in a tone barely above a whisper and admitted, "Brutus dropped down a key."

"Of course he did."

"What?"

Ray's voice took on an impatient quality, "How do you think I found you, Ember? This building is surrounded by crows. It looks like something out of a horror film."

"Oh, we're definitely in a horror movie."

"Slide the key under the door so I can see if it works. It's worth a shot."

Ember crouched down and was about to slide the key under the door, but her muscles grew tense. Could she really trust Ray? What did she really know about him? For all she knew, he was working with her dad.

"Did you hear me, Ember?"

"I heard you," Ember crouched down and placed her face against the frigid ground. She could just make out the bottom of Ray's shoes. The gap was large enough that she could slide the key underneath and watch him walk away if he decided not to release her from her prison. Of course, that was only if the key worked.

Ember sucked in a deep breath and said her deepest fear out loud, "What if you betray me?"

Ray sighed, the sound appeared to match the exhaustion in his soul. He did something that managed to shock Ember to her core. Instead of growing frustrated or visibly angry, Ray simply took several steps away from the door. She watched with a sense of detached fascination as Ray kept his distance and explained, "I can't make you trust me, Ember. In all honesty, you probably have very few reasons to feel safe with me. It's your choice."

Ember felt compelled to watch as Ray took one final generous step away from the door. She could barely see the toes of his shoes from such a distance. Ember could still sense his presence as faintly as she could see the outline of his boots.

    Nervous energy swirled around in the pit of Ember's belly as she decided what to do. How could she possibly make such a choice? Then again, did she have another option? Not really.

    She closed her eyes and sent a silent prayer to her madre y abuela. Por favor, ayúda me.

    Ember opened her eyes and slid the key under the door. She watched as the key glinted against the final strands of light and then momentarily disappeared from view as it passed to the other side. The sound of metal sliding against the cold floor was the only sign that she had ever held the key in the first place.

    "Please don't fuck me."

Chapter 50

"I heard that."

"Good, you were supposed to."

"Are you always such a smart ass?"

"Are you always so damn slow opening doors?"

Ray grunted from the other side. The two giant doors groaned under the pressure of Ray's force. After a few tense moments, Ray released a curse.

Ember scrunched her eyes shut and bit her lower lip. He didn't need to say it. Ember already knew. The key didn't work.

A distant rumble tickled the back of Ember's awareness. Gravel crunched somewhere near the side of the building. It was definitely the sound of a larger car. Probably an extermination van.

"He's coming back, Ray. You need to leave. Call for backup. Hide. You just can't be here when he gets here."

"Okay, I have an idea. Do you trust me? I need to get him to unlock the door before I can save the mayor."

Ember was still pressed against the cool ground. She could barely discern Ray's shoes as he anxiously shifted from one foot to the other. Ember lightly pounded her forehead against the ground in frustration. She instantly regretted the action as her injured head screamed in protest.

"Do I have another option?"

"I'm taking that as a yes."

"Yes. Come back soon."

"That's the idea."

Ember watched as Ray's shoes quickly disappeared from sight. Her heart pounded in her chest and threatened to explode into a million tiny pieces. She stood on shaky legs and decided to sit next to the mayor. The mayor was still on the floor, but her breathing was growing labored. Her head was still positioned on the ground. Her mouth was less than a centimeter from the edge of the water. Ember hoped that she'd be able to stall while protecting the mayor from her so-called father.

The chains rattled and swiftly fell to the ground as the two double-doors swiftly flung open. Ember was huddled in the corner right next to the mayor. She looked up and the blood instantly drained from her face.

The look in his eyes was vacant as a cruel smile played along the edges of his lips. Her father cocked his head to the side and chided, "That wasn't a very smart idea."

"What?"

"You're untied."

Chapter 51

Shit.

In the blink of an eye, Bill charged across the room. He easily closed the distance as Ember struggled to stand and move out of his way.

He was too fast.

Pain erupted behind the back of Ember's eyes. Bursts of light exploded behind her closed lids as she struggled to comprehend what had happened. In a matter of moments, Bill had managed to hit her across the face with a wrench.

Fury consumed Ember. A rage like she had never felt before flared to life. She despised this man, blood or not. He was a merciless killer. A monster. She glanced at the mayor for less than a second before she finally made her decision.

She feigned to the left and then quickly outmaneuvered her much heavier adversary. She sprinted out the door. Ember ran out of the unlocked door like a bat out of hell. Her feet pounded against the floor as she sped down the lengthy corridor and pushed open a door. The scent of damp grass and dirt instantly greeted her senses. She noticed that she had indeed been held captive in the abandoned section of the hospital. After gathering her bearings, she took off in the direction of the lake. Heavy footsteps pounded only a few paces behind, but Ember refused to look back. She needed to focus on every step as her limbs stretched into the future. One slight fumble and she knew that her fate was sealed. She had refused to listen to the requests of a madman and now she was also on his list of victims.

A distant gunshot erupted into the air and urged Ember on. Ray had hopefully managed to break the glass.

Bill roared, realizing that he'd been tricked into leaving the hospital, "You should have just listened to me! We could have celebrated you joining the family business. Instead, you crossed my path just like your mother."

The fury from earlier had never disappeared, instead it continued to reach a steady boil. Ember's rage pushed her to run faster as her mind sprinted at the speed of light to form an idea. She was closer to the lake. The ground grew more forgiving and the plants appeared more vibrant. The colors around the area were brighter and the air was unusually quiet. It was as if nature was waiting. Waiting for Ember to exact her retribution. Ember could hear Bill shouting from a distance, but she ignored it. From the sound of his voice, she was gaining a lead. She mentally thanked abuela for forcing her to participate in track and field during high school.

In the back of her mind, a passionate, maternal voice whispered, *corre*. The voice turned into a chant that intertwined into every inch of Ember's soul. She slid down the embankment and noticed the pile of rope left out for one of the patrol boats. She quickly kicked around the dirt to camouflage the base of the staked rope. She wrapped the free end of the rope around her waist and doubled-knotted it. She didn't have time to check the integrity of her work as she sprinted into the water. The cold robbed Ember's lungs of air. Luckily, the righteous anger in her chest kept her warm. She swam into the lake and turned to look at the shore.

Bill escaped the tree line. He looked around until his gaze found Ember's face. Even in the dwindling light, Ember could see the vacancy in his soulless eyes. She had never considered herself religious, but Bill appeared to be as close to the devil as possible. He had remained hidden in plain sight for years. Managing to silently ruin people's lives without ever having a single finger pointed in his direction. Until now.

"Come out of the water so we can talk. We are family, after all."

Ember treaded water as goose pimples bloomed along her frigid body. She shivered and shook her head. Ember realized that it was quickly growing too dark for Bill to notice the subtle movement.

She sucked in a deep breath and screamed, "Never! I'm glad my mom left you. You're a nobody. A nothing. A powerless coward. Look, you're even afraid of a little water."

"I'm not a coward! I've made people beg," Bill ped closer to the water. He approached from an angle that it impossible for him to notice the thin rope that linked to the land. He stomped closer to the body of water and halted just at the edge. His chest rapidly rose and fell in what Ember could only assume was anger. Of course, his anger was only brought on by shame. He was too small of a man to know what the burn of actual injustice felt like. Instead, he only knew the anger and shame tied to his fragile and currently crumbling ego.

    Ember swam closer to the middle of the lake. The current grew in intensity. It was as if the lake was slowly waking up. Growing aware of its next potential meal. Ember shouted, "You don't have the courage to drown me with your bare hands! That's why you always hid behind your twisted inventions and tools. You're too scared to look me in the eyes."

    Bill roared and sloppily stumbled into the water. Spray flew into the air and danced with the pale moonlight as he began to swim to Ember.

    The water began to churn. A faint spinning sound caught Ember's attention. Her eyes widened in shock as a cyclone of spiraling water appeared to drift in her direction. Rope or not, Ember knew that she had to move. She had no clue how deep the lake actually was. It was possible that she'd end up pulled down to the very bottom in a furious tornado of liquid and drown. The rope could only do so much. She was tethered to the land, but that would only help people dredge up her drowned corpse. She wouldn't be strong enough to swim out of its grasp.

Bill hadn't noticed the shift in the water. His entire focus was directed on Ember as he weakly swam in her general direction. He was getting closer and Ember had to fight her instincts to stay put. She continued to tread water as she watched him approach.

Suddenly, the water swallowed him whole. One second his face was contorted in a furious clumsy panic and the next, Ember could only see his feet as he capsized under the silent surface. The water spun in a circle and Ember swore that she could see Bill as he moved to the bottom of the lake. One hand outstretched to the surface, but doomed to steadily move deeper into the abyss.

Exhaustion clawed at Ember's bones. She struggled to keep swimming. The lake's current was now impossible to ignore. She gave up and decided to attempt to pull her body to shore. Her arms burned as she gripped the rope and tried to inch her way to land.

Suddenly, the rope began to move closer to shore. Someone was pulling her in. Her hands stung as the rough rope cut into her hands and she fought to stay awake.

Her toes mercifully touched the bottom of the lake. Ember cried out in relief as the rope around her waist steadily 'er to shore. Drenched and shaking, Ember looked up of the person that had just saved her life. Her 'd together as her body furiously shook against the re.

Chapter 52

"Nurse Kit?"

"Yes. Good to see that the massive lump on your head hasn't rendered you useless," The sharp words starkly contrasted the turmoil and concern obviously painted against the older woman's features. Her fingers shook as she placed a reassuring hand against Ember's shoulder.

Ember struggled to catch her breath as exhaustion hammered into her senses like a battering ram. The faint sound of sirens howled through the unforgiving February breeze. For some reason, Nurse Kit's features seemed oddly familiar. Ember struggled to place where she had seen such a face. She knew that it had to be from somewhere.

Realization hit Ember between her eyes and burned its way through her brain like a bullet. She gasped, "You're Hallie's mother."

Five letters. One simple word. In the end, a single name that had so obviously been the center of Nurse Kit's world. The woman's face crumbled into a mask of despair. Her brows pulled together as her lower lip quivered in agony. She released a heartbreaking wail that pierced the once heavy silence. It sounded as if someone had managed to reach into her chest and pulled out her heart. Perhaps, in a way, someone had already done just that.

    Shaky arms embraced Ember's body. Ember reacted on instinct alone. The pain was too much to be felt alone. She gripped Nurse Kit and the two clung to each other as the mud wrapped around their ankles while the rain cleansed their skin. Time had no meaning. For just a few heart beats, the two women were one, mourning and grieving an indescribable loss. Bearing witness to the cruelty of man from the temporary safety of a continually sinking embankment. Eventually, they would need to climb out and stand on solid ground. For a moment they simply embraced. Felt all the grief and the years of torment that were too heavy and cumbersome for the tongue to fully express. Their movements were swift and concise where words were clumsy and prolonged.

    Eventually, the duo moved. They genuflected near the bottom of the bridge. Ember's mouth felt dry even though her entire body was drenched to the core. She managed to mutter out, "I was his executioner."

    A steady hand rested against Ember's shoulder, "No, you were simply providing justice."

    The sirens were closer, but Ember's attention remained transfixed on the water. It swirled in an unforgiving pattern as if rejoicing in a well-earned victory.

Chapter 53

"It's stupid."

"How do you know it's stupid if you haven't even seen it?"

"Because I can feel that it's heavy and impractical."

"Take a look," Ray arched a single brow in a direct challenge to Ember's bullheaded remarks.

Ember released a dramatic sigh and reluctantly walked over to the mirror. She was sure that the jacket looked ridiculous. It was one of Ray's. None of her jackets were able to accommodate the tight cast on her wrist. The stitches on her head and the obvious bruising along her ribs made her a sight for sore eyes. However, once Ember reached the long mirror in her hallway, she found that she was at a loss for words. The oversized jacket actually looked really nice. She bit her lower lip, unwilling to admit defeat, but it was too late. Ray had already noticed that she agreed with his assessment. She looked nice. The jacket looked as if it had always belonged in her closet. An edgy comfortable compliment to her long flowing dress.

For the first time in about a decade, she was heading out to celebrate her birthday. Ray had promised a quiet meal at the diner and then an obligatory celebratory cake with Nurse Kit, Donna, and Sherriff Art. Ember had made it a point to complain and stall, but secretly she was excited to do something festive. The wound on her head and the bruises along her ribs were all very much real, but she found the invisible scars from her father much more concerning. Ember knew that she needed to make it a point to go out early and often to avoid the temptation of becoming a shut-in.

"Let's feed the birds and then we can go."

For once, Ray didn't protest. Instead, he reached into the cabinet and pulled out an expensive bag of new corn with one hand. He nodded in agreement as he said, "Sure."

Now it was Ember's turn to look skeptical. She tilted her head to the side as she inspected Ray. Had he been abducted by aliens? Why was he being so patient about her precious birds?

As if he could read her mind, Ray simply shrugged his good shoulder as he clutched the bag of corn in his capable hand and explained, "Birds of a feather. They helped me find you, Ember. I'm more than happy to feed the little pests."

A slow smile crept along the edges of Ember's lips as she crept closer. She leaned onto the tips of her toes and hovered a few inches away from Ray's lips. In a voice barely above a whisper, she asked, "Detective Ray, are you feeling grateful for my perfect little murder?"

"Absolutely. Heck, I'll feed the crows every day from now on. I don't mind."

Ember laughed, "I didn't know that you felt so strongly about my feathered friends."

Ray closed the distance so that their lips were almost touching. Any closer and their worlds would collide. Ray stood firm as he looked deep into Ember's eyes and vowed, "I feel strongly about you, Ember Lopez."

Ember closed the distance. Their lips danced at a leisurely pace to a song that only they could hear. Eventually, Ray pulled away. He rested his forehead against Ember's. Ember appreciated the welcomed silence. It was a silence full of inarticulable meaning.

Eventually, Ray pulled away as he hefted the bag of corn higher onto his uninjured shoulder and headed out to feed her crows.

Chapter 54

A month had managed to pass in relative anonymity. Ember was still licking her emotional wounds, but she was healing. Nurse Kit had become an unexpected lunch partner. Her sharp tongue and witty remarks managed to quell the fears that seemed to still lurk in the back of Ember's mind.

Ember exited the hospital cafeteria after a particularly unsatisfying tuna sandwich and headed down to the lobby. Ray stood next to the entrance. An impish smirk overtook his face once he noticed Ember's approach. Ember returned a small relaxed smile as she swiftly closed the distance.

"What did you find?"

"I didn't find anything, yet. It's just a hunch."

The two walked outside as Ember led the way to the abandoned hospital wing. She wondered if it had ever needed an exterminator in the first place. Was it possible that her father had simply planted the ants in an attempt to gain access to an impressive amount of unused space? The possibility seemed only too real.

Ember took one step after the other as she clutched the key that Brutus had given her. She looked at Ray from the corner of her eyes and noticed that he likely felt equally as tense. The two entered the long empty hospital wing and Ember walked over to an unremarkable supply closet. She paused and then tossed the key between her palms.

"What are you thinking?"

"I'm thinking that it's a little suspicious that Bill's house was raided, but they couldn't find more than $10 to his name. He had to have stored it somewhere. I'm willing to bet that it's around here."

Ray nodded his head and watched from a few steps away as Ember's hand tentatively hovered over the handle of the janitor's closet. She nervously licked her lower lip and explained, "I did some research on this key. It's old and was designed for doors made in the early 1900s."

"Like the hospital," Ray replied.

"Yep. I figured that it wouldn't unlock an obvious room, but a supply room that everyone would ignore. Somewhere easy to hide. A place that's hidden in plain sight."

"You're stalling."

"Damn you," Ember cursed at Ray as her sweaty palms placed the key into the door. It was a perfect fit. The lock turned and the door swung open.

Ember stepped back and her jaw nearly hit the floor as surprise rendered her momentarily speechless. Ray stepped closer and gave a low whistle. The supply closet was loaded with an assortment of dollar bills and checks.

A small embellished swan head rested on a stack of cash. A sharp cry escaped the back of Ember's throat as she stared in horror at the personal belongings. Ray instantly stepped closer and his warmth seeped into Ember's back as she continued her inspection. He placed a comforting palm against the curve of Ember's hip.

"We divide it evenly and make sure it goes to the families."

Ray spluttered out, "But you don't have a job, Ember. This could help."

Ember tilted her head to the side and narrowed her eyes, daring him to continue. Satisfied, Ember added, "This doesn't belong to me. Besides, I've been thinking of going into a different line of business."

Ray grunted, "Really? Like what?"

"I know this detective, but I feel that he'd be better off working with a partner. He doesn't exactly have the best record, so he's currently being kept on a suffocatingly tight leash."

"Is that so?"

"Yep. I would like to partner with this detective and start our own detective agency. I want to help people find their missing loved ones. In private. Off the record. Without a podcast."

Ray held her gaze and regarded her with a calculating silence. He carefully weighed her words, searching for even the slightest sign of a joke. Of course, he found none. Ember was absolutely serious.

"That's one hell of a way to ask me to go into business with you."

Ember placed a hand against Ray's chest and stood on the tips of her toes. She looked deep into Ray's stormy gaze and asked, "What do you say, partner?"

"I think you're going to be a pain in my ass."

"Sure."

Ray continued, "A partner that isn't a pain in the ass isn't a partner worth having."

"I'm taking that as a compliment."

"It was meant as one."

El Fin.

Camille Cabrera

Camille Cabrera is a #1 top selling American mystery author. She specializes in sub genres such as noir and suspense. Her works often involve complicated and controversial female protagonists. She takes great pride to create works that center around a specific holiday in order to contrast the familiar celebration with the unknown shroud of death.

Her most recent novel, CHRONOMETER, reached the top 10 on Amazon on two different charts. CHRONOMETER was one of her most challenging works to craft given the extensive artistic risks. Her upcoming novel, BELOW THE WATER, is slated for release in December 2023.

More Books by Camille Cabrera:

Catalina's Tide

The Rule of Three

Chronometer

Below The Water

Printed in the USA
CPSIA information can be obtained
at www.ICGtesting.com
LVHW061050200624
783566LV00017B/412